Cold to the Bone

Starlight glistened off the naked man's scrawny frame as he bounded into the oaks and ash . . . Longarm's breath smoked in the frigid air. He raised the rifle and fired three quick rounds toward the naked man's pale, scissoring feet.

The whip-cracks of the rifle reports rocked the cold, quiet night. One of the slugs spanged off a rock near Bone's left foot. Bone yelped, careened to one side, and ran on. Beneath the Winchester's dying echoes, Longarm could hear the man's raspy breaths, grunts, and groans.

If Bone was like most Western men, north of his boots he was tough as rawhide, able to endure . . . discomfort. But his feet, accustomed to the protection of cotton and leather, were likely tender as a newborn baby's ass. Longarm winced as he listened to the man's dwindling grunts and painful sighs, imagining the burrs and sharp rocks biting into the undersides of the outlaw's tender dogs.

Not only that, but it was damn cold. Even a wizened-up old mountain man would die out here within the hour—just curl up under a pine and slip off into the next world . . .

DON'T MISS THESE
ALL-ACTION WESTERN SERIES
FROM THE BERKLEY PUBLISHING GROUP

THE GUNSMITH by J. R. Roberts

Clint Adams was a legend among lawmen, outlaws, and ladies. They called him . . . the Gunsmith.

LONGARM by Tabor Evans

The popular long-running series about Deputy U.S. Marshal Custis Long—his life, his loves, his fight for justice.

SLOCUM by Jake Logan

Today's longest-running action Western. John Slocum rides a deadly trail of hot blood and cold steel.

BUSHWHACKERS by B. J. Lanagan

An action-packed series by the creators of Longarm! The rousing adventures of the most brutal gang of cutthroats ever assembled—Quantrill's Raiders.

DIAMONDBACK by Guy Brewer

Dex Yancey is Diamondback, a Southern gentleman turned con man when his brother cheats him out of the family fortune. Ladies love him. Gamblers hate him. But nobody pulls one over on Dex . . .

WILDGUN by Jack Hanson

The blazing adventures of mountain man Will Barlow—from the creators of Longarm!

TEXAS TRACKER by Tom Calhoun

J. T. Law: the most relentless—and dangerous—manhunter in all Texas. Where sheriffs and posses fail, he's the best man to bring in the most vicious outlaws—for a price.

TABOR EVANS

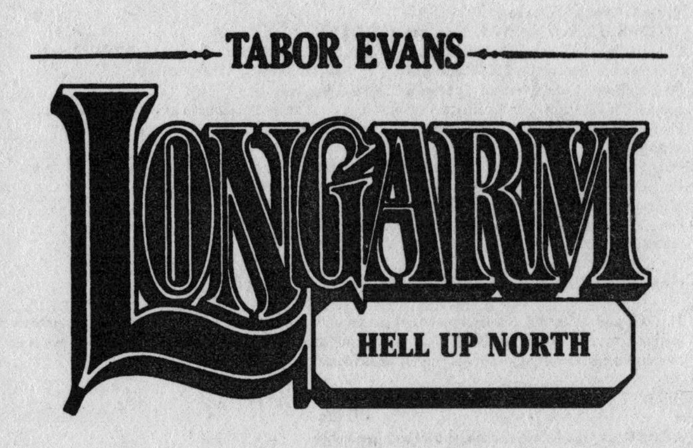

JOVE BOOKS, NEW YORK

THE BERKLEY PUBLISHING GROUP
Published by the Penguin Group
Penguin Group (USA) Inc.
375 Hudson Street, New York, New York 10014, USA
Penguin Group (Canada), 90 Eglinton Avenue East, Suite 700, Toronto, Ontario M4P 2Y3, Canada
(a division of Pearson Penguin Canada Inc.)
Penguin Books Ltd., 80 Strand, London WC2R 0RL, England
Penguin Group Ireland, 25 St. Stephen's Green, Dublin 2, Ireland (a division of Penguin Books Ltd.)
Penguin Group (Australia), 250 Camberwell Road, Camberwell, Victoria 3124, Australia
(a division of Pearson Australia Group Pty. Ltd.)
Penguin Books India Pvt. Ltd., 11 Community Centre, Panchsheel Park, New Delhi—110 017, India
Penguin Group (NZ), 67 Apollo Drive, Rosedale, North Shore 0632, New Zealand
(a division of Pearson New Zealand Ltd.)
Penguin Books (South Africa) (Pty.) Ltd., 24 Sturdee Avenue, Rosebank, Johannesburg 2196, South Africa

Penguin Books Ltd., Registered Offices: 80 Strand, London WC2R 0RL, England

HELL UP NORTH

A Jove Book / published by arrangement with the author

PRINTING HISTORY
Jove edition / April 2009

Cover illustration by Miro Sinovcic.

For information, address: The Berkley Publishing Group,
a division of Penguin Group (USA) Inc.,
375 Hudson Street, New York, New York 10014.

ISBN: 978-0-515-14607-3

JOVE®
Jove Books are published by The Berkley Publishing Group,
a division of Penguin Group (USA) Inc.,
375 Hudson Street, New York, New York 10014.
JOVE® is a registered trademark of Penguin Group (USA) Inc.
The "J" design is a trademark of Penguin Group (USA) Inc.

PRINTED IN THE UNITED STATES OF AMERICA

10 9 8 7 6 5 4 3 2 1

Chapter 1

Deputy U.S. Marshal Custis Long put his rented pinto up a high, grassy hill, letting the horse pick its own way around scattered bur oaks, sumac, ash, and juneberry. He held his Winchester carbine across his saddlebows, edgily caressing the trigger with his gloved index finger and frowning at the fresh horse apples scattered amongst the buckbrush and snowberry.

It was a cold autumn dusk on the high Dakota plains.

Grizzlies prowled the river bottoms, wolves howled on the tablelands, and the first stars glistened like polished pearls above the violet eastern horizon.

The lawman, known as Longarm to friend and foe, dug the scarf up from under the collar of his heavy buckskin, fleece-lined mackinaw and tightened it under his jaws. The breeze had one hell of an edge to it. Like a cold, sharp knife. He'd forgotten how cold it could get up here, northwest of Bismarck, only a stone's throw from the broad, deep Missouri River that was already starting to freeze up around its edges.

As he raised the scarf, he gave it a sniff. Damn, if he

couldn't still smell the perfume of Cynthia Larimer in the loosely woven, teal wool.

The beguiling niece of General William Larimer, Denver's founding father and one of the five wealthiest men in Colorado Territory, had given the scarf to Longarm the night before he'd embarked upon his current assignment—to run down the five men who'd killed three deputy U.S. marshals out of Helena, Montana Territory, and who'd also left a trail of raped and battered women in their bank-robbing, stagecoach ravaging sweep across the north country.

It wasn't Longarm's territory, but he'd been called up from the Sixth District in Denver to take over the hunt when five marshals out of Bismarck had found themselves hoofing a cold trail and were unable to beat it warm again.

Cynthia had presented the scarf to Longarm at the unlikeliest of moments—while she'd straddled the federal lawman atop a silky bobcat hide in front of the snapping hearth in her candlelit boudoir, in the Larimer's sprawling mansion, with Longarm's rock-hard shaft angling up deep into the girl's wet, fiery core.

"Oh, no, Custis!" she'd cried, sucking a sharp breath through her teeth. Leaning forward, the otherworldly, black-haired, blue-eyed vixen buried her fingers a good two inches into the lawman's slablike pectorals and snaked her feet taut around his knees. "Ooo-eeee . . . no! Not *yet*!"

"For the love of all that's holy, girl—how long you think I can keep this up?" Longarm rasped, gritting his teeth and trying to keep his eyes off the girl's creamy breasts bulging out from between her long, slender arms, the nipples like pink, tender rosebuds angling slightly off center. If he stared at those magnificent orbs too long, he was sure to blow his load. "I'm only human fer Christ-fuckin'-sakes!"

"Let's take a break for a minute, Custis. Maybe hum a little church tune, huh?"

Cynthia let her bottom sink down to his thighs, and the hair on the back of his neck pricked as he pushed farther into her, her insides grasping his cock like an iron fist.

"Or, how 'bout . . ." She reached toward the hearth, shoved a newspaper aside, and grabbed a rectangular, gold-wrapped box. "Here. This is for you. I saw it in a shop just after I got off the train from San Francisco. It'll keep you warm on your trip to the north country. Open it." She spoke slowly, narrowing her harrowing blue eyes at him, as though she were trying to hypnotize him. "Think about the scarf. Not me. No, no, no. Not me or what we're doing. Just think about the scarf."

"The scarf . . . okay, I'll try," Longarm croaked, shoving up onto his elbows. He plucked the box out of the girl's hands and quickly unwrapped it. Seldom had he felt so miserable. They'd been going at it like a couple of back-alley dogs for nigh on thirty minutes, after they'd taken a bath together in the general's own private tub, and she wanted him to pull back from the very edge *now*?

Longarm's heart thudded and his shaft swelled with rapturous torture as, with slightly shaking hands, he tossed the bow and the wrapping paper aside and lifted the lid from the box. He'd plucked the scarf from the box, tossed the box aside, and extended the scarf out in front of him.

"Well, lookee there," he croaked, trying to sound grateful. "Sure enough it's a scarf—a green one!"

"It's teal, and woven from the very best wool."

"Teal it is." Longarm caressed his cheek with the scarf. "Ah, that's a dandy-feelin' wool, too. I can tell it's right up there with the very best a feller could find without his trampin' all the way to Wyoming for it and buying it fresh off the ole ewe's back!" He was trying so hard not to blow his load that it was hard to sound anything except distracted and miserable.

The girl laughed huskily. "Let me try it on."

She grabbed the scarf out of his hands and wrapped it around her neck. Giggling, stretching her rich lips back from snow-white teeth and showing the pink tip of her tongue, she wound the ends of the scarf around her full, porcelain-pale breasts, encircling each fully and causing them to swell delectably, the rosebud nipples aimed at the ceiling.

"How do I look, Custis?"

Longarm traced her breasts with his gaze. His temples throbbed and his cheek twitched. Sweat dribbled down his neck.

She smiled delightfully down at him, poking her tongue slightly out.

"Miss Cynthia, I do believe you're purposely trying to torture me into a fuckin' heart stroke!" Longarm bellowed through gritted teeth.

"Oh, Custis!" Cynthia screeched as he bounded up to a sitting position and flung the girl onto her back, cushioning her head with his hands and somehow still keeping his shaft rammed firmly up into her core.

She yelped as he jacked her legs up with his arms, until her knees were nearly shoved back to her jaws and her feet dangled out beside his shoulders. Longarm backed out of the girl quickly, then rose up onto his toes and, watching her eyes snap wide with terror mixed with euphoria, drove himself so far home he thought for a second he'd nail her to the floor.

"Cust-isssssss!" she cried as he loosed his load with the fervor of a nickel-plated, freshly loaded Gatling gun fired by a mad, syphilitic killer.

Longarm snorted at the memory and swung down from the big pinto. Cynthia. *Damn, old son,* he told himself, *you best get that little filly out of your head right quick.* Right unprofessional . . . a lawman thinking of fucking when he's so close to the three killers he's been tracking up one hill in this soon-to-be-frozen wasteland and down another for two, going on three weeks now that their horse shit is still warm.

Kneeling, he dropped the apple he'd tested between thumb and index finger and pulled on his glove. He tied the pinto to a branch of an ash sapling, then stole through the scattered shrubs to the top of the hill and hunkered down between a mossy boulder and a chokecherry bush.

Below, the little roadhouse he'd heard about in town nestled at the base of the hill—a two-story log-and-stone hovel with a steeply pitched roof, better to parry the heavy snows that fell in this bitter country, and a large fieldstone hearth climbing the left wall.

Between the hill and the roadhouse lay a small lean-to shelter and a chopping block with a long-handled hatchet embedded in it. A sprawling cottonwood stood left of the block, and a deer carcass hung from a low branch, turning this way and that in the chill autumn breeze.

Lights shone in the roadhouse's sashed windows, and a piano's muffled patter seeped through the stout, log walls.

Longarm lifted the collar of his sheepskin mackinaw, pulled the brim of his snuff brown hat lower on his forehead, gripped his Winchester in both gloved hands, and started down the hill. He took long, ground-eating strides. His low-heeled cavalry boots slipped slightly in the dry brown grass, but he made fast work of the slope and was hunkered up against the roadhouse's back wall in less than a minute.

He could hear the piano a little clearer now though the walls still muffled it. Beneath the piano's tinny clatter, bed-springs sounded as though they were getting a good work-out. A woman laughed raucously—the voice of a crusty, lusty old bobcat laughing hysterically at a bawdy joke.

Probably the madam of the place. Longarm had learned in town that the Sand Creek Roadhouse, as this place was called, had actually been a small ranch at one time, converted to a brothel when the rancher died and the widow decided to start running girls instead of cattle for a living.

One of the killers Longarm was tracking was known to fancy one of the girls here, and he couldn't keep himself away when he found himself anywhere near, dodging American lawmen or Canadian Mounties.

The madam's choice to run a roadhouse instead of a ranch seemed right practical to Longarm, who believed that, like water, a person should always choose the path of least resistance . . . as long as he or she did so within the law, of course.

Time to get this show on the road, he thought, lowering his coat collar to free up the movement of his neck. Cynthia's faint perfume wafted into his nostrils again, giving his loins a preternatural prod. If all went well here in the next ten minutes, he should be on his way back to Denver first thing in the morning.

He edged around the corner of the roadhouse. His boot kicked something. There was a glassy thud and rasp followed by a faint chugging sound. Sucking a sharp breath through gritted teeth, Longarm froze mid-step and looked down.

A bottle lay in the spindly grass and gravel, dark liquid leaking from the open mouth. Someone had likely left the bottle here at the corner of the roadhouse when they'd come out to take a piss and had forgotten to pick it up again.

If someone had been out here just now, they probably would have heard that. Longarm castigated himself. *Be aware of everything around you, fool. Even whiskey bottles. You're alone here, and it would take only one Cynthia-Larimer-clouded thought to get you beefed good and true.* These killers would throw his carcass so deep down a ravine or an old mine chute that no one would ever know what had happened to him except a handful of wolves and maybe a coyote or two.

Longarm's boss, Chief Marshal Billy Vail, wouldn't have even a badge to bury.

Longarm stepped over the bottle and stole along the side of the roadhouse. He stopped at the first of two windows on this side and doffed his hat. He edged a look around the window casing and a swatch of gauzy, pink curtain into the lantern-lit room.

The lawman hiked a chestnut brow over a deep-set brown steel blue eye and spread his brown mustache in a bemused smile.

On a brass bad, a chubby, redheaded girl and a scrawny younker with long, stringy blond hair and a spade beard were frolicking doggy style. The girl knelt belly down on the bed, ass in the air, her pale, plump hands clutching the brass spools in the headboard as though she were clutching the rail of a storm-battered schooner, fearful of being swept into a roaring, inky black sea.

The younker, whom Longarm recognized from the likeness on a wanted dodger as Erroll "Bone" McCluskey, knelt between the girl's thighs, and gripping her hip bones, drew her large, plump butt back and forth against his crotch, making the bedsprings sing, causing the headboard to hammer the plankboard wall, and evoking a throaty "Ahh!" from the redhead each time the kid jerked her back against him, yelling, "There! How's that, bitch? Huh? How you like *that*?"

Longarm ducked under the window and continued moving along the wall, squeezing his rifle as he headed for the front door, muttering, "Doesn't seem to me she's all that crazy for it, Bone . . ."

Chapter 2

Still hearing the bed's squawk and Bone McCluskey's guttural exclamations as well as an added murmur of conversation from nearer the front of the lodge, Longarm stepped around the building's front corner and mounted the whorehouse's stoop.

The floor of the stoop was constructed of whipsawed pine planks, most of which had seen far better days. Several were broken. Several more were missing. Longarm kept his eyes on the floor as he ducked under a front window and stole along toward the door, careful he didn't step through a gap and drop to the ground two feet below.

On the door side of the window, he dropped to a knee, and edged a look inside. This window had only a tattered flour sack for curtains. Beyond them and the flyspecked, dust-smeared glass, he saw a table around which three men sat playing cards.

On a cot near the back and beyond a fire dancing in the large fieldstone hearth, another man and a round-faced brunette were lying on a large cot covered with buffalo robes, sort of snuggling and playing giggly-goo. They were both flushed and perspiring and grinning like the cat that ate the bluebird.

The girl lay beside the man, Sneaky Pete Whalen, with her pointy, little breasts exposed. Sneaky Pete was running a berry up and down the whore's cleavage, a smoky grin on his broad, bony face, his thin brown hair hanging in his eyes. The girl lay on one elbow, grinning lasciviously as her hand moved under the robes down around Sneaky Pete's waist.

On the left side of the shadowy room cluttered with odds and ends of furniture and miscellaneous clothing and tack hanging from ceiling joists, a stout woman in a shapeless dress worked at a large, black range. A loosely rolled quirley dangled from her lips.

She had a fist on a large, round hip as she moved a spatula around in a cast-iron pan. She turned her head back and forth between the table and the pan as her lips moved nonstop. Her back was facing Longarm, so he couldn't make out much of what she was saying, but she seemed to be rambling on about everything from the weather to the quality of the fishing in a nearby lake, cracking a joke now and then and throwing her head back to loose her booming, masculine laughter at the low-timbered ceiling.

None of the men at the table paid any attention to her, grimly absorbed as they were in their card game and whiskey. The two on the cot certainly weren't following her conversation; in fact, the brunette's head had disappeared under the buffalo robes, and Sneaky Pete Whalen had leaned his own head back against the wall. His lower jaw hung nearly to his chest, and his mouth corners rose with an ethereal smile.

Longarm didn't see a gun anywhere near Sneaky Pete, though he probably had one under the robes. The appropriately named outlaw, cousin of Bone McCluskey, was wanted in nearly every Western territory, and it wasn't likely he'd ever stray far from a firearm. Longarm had to assume he had at least one pistol near to hand.

From what the lawman could see of the four cardplayers, they were all armed, as well. He saw one bone-gripped Peacemaker on the table near an ashtray in which a stout cigar smoldered. Against the opposite side of the table leaned a Winchester saddle-ring carbine. He could also make out two filled holsters thonged low on two of the men's thighs. One was a Bisley .44—he noted the distinctive curve of the British-made hogleg's handle, as well as its scrolled nickel plating.

The owner of that prized piece would be Bryce Coyle, said to be a nephew of the territorial governor of Nevada. Coyle was rumored to have shot a deputy U.S. marshal through the back of the lawman's throat with a gun fitting the Bisley's description, at a stage stop near Fort Pierre.

Longarm pulled away from the window and drew a deep breath. This wasn't going to be a July Fourth ice-cream social. He was facing as woolly a crew of curly wolves as he'd ever taken down. But it was going to be a relief to him and every other badge toter west of the Mississippi to have them all under lock and key . . . or nibbling sage roots, whichever the case might be.

He started to rise. A board creaked under his left boot. He rose more slowly, gritting his teeth, the board creaking too softly now to be heard inside above the constant whoosh of the chill breeze under the overhanging eaves.

He tiptoed over to the door, squared his shoulders, and taking the Winchester in his right hand and pointing the barrel at the door's vertical planks, slid his left hand toward the latch.

A board chirped beneath his right boot.

A voice inside the cabin said, "What was that?"

"What was what?"

"Somethin's out there!"

Cursing under his breath, Longarm took the Winchester in both hands, raised his right boot, and kicked the door. It blew open with a bark and slammed against the wall, making the whole room jump and causing a can to hit the floor with a clatter. The metal latch and splinters from the casing sprayed in all directions.

"Law!" Longarm shouted above the killers' surprised exclamations, taking one step into the cabin, raising the rifle to his shoulder, and thumbing back the off-cocked hammer. *"Reach for the rafters or die where you stand, you fork-tailed sons o' bitches!"*

The ultimatum had as much effect as a heathen's prayer against a cyclone. Chairs flew as the four cardplayers bolted straight up, flinging exasperated looks at the suddenly open doorway filled with a mustachioed lawman in a snuff brown hat and buckskin mackinaw aiming a Winchester '73 from his broad right shoulder, squinting a steel blue eye down the octagonal barrel as, choosing a target, he lined up the sights.

Longarm squeezed the trigger as Bryce Coyle swung toward him with a fistful of silver-plated Bisley.

Ka-boom!

The Winchester's slug drilled a quarter-sized hole through Coyle's forehead, just right of his nose. Coyle's face went slack as, firing the Bisley into the rafters over Longarm's head, he flew back into the man who'd been sitting on the table's right side.

"Son of a *bitch*!" screamed the man on the far side of the table, raising the bone-gripped Peacemaker and grimacing around the stogie clamped in the side of his mouth.

Ka-boom!

As Longarm's slug took the man through his chest, just above the silver crucifix dangling down his open shirt, and punched him straight back toward the rear of the room, Longarm ejected the smoking shell and seated a fresh one in the breech. He triggered another round, sending the man on the table's left side spinning and screaming and triggering a shot from his own Colt into the fireplace on the room's right side.

The whore on the cot screamed. The big woman at the range shouted, "Oh, ya lousy bastards—don't shoot up my *place*!"

Her words were virtually drowned by Longarm's belching Winchester, which dispatched not only the third gun-wielding killer but the fourth man, Sneaky Pete Whalen, as the broad-faced outlaw bolted out from under the buffalo robes, as naked as the day he was born, his wet, red dong still half erect, and raising a Smith & Wesson saddle-ring revolver in each fist as he laughed bizarrely and bellowed, *"Die, lawdog, die, ya son of a bitch!"*

Both his pistols belched smoke and flames simultaneously. But Longarm's own two slugs, triggered a half second before, nudged Sneaky Pete's shots wide as they plowed through the man's hairless chest and his flat right cheek respectively.

Movement low around the table caught Longarm's attention as he jerked the cocking lever down and a smoking shell casing arced over his shoulder and out the open door to clatter onto the porch behind him. There was a grunt, and one of the gamblers showed his unshaven face above his chair.

It was Phil DeRosso. He was known as the Caveman because that's just how he looked, as though no time had elapsed between Phil and the club-wielding, cave-dwelling hordes of many thousand years ago. His thin, brown hair was plastered across his broad pate, and his thick lips shivered as blood poured over the lower one to dribble down his weak, furry chin.

Longarm aimed the Winchester, angling it low as the killer—the coldest one of the group, known to piss on his victims—pushed up off a chair, fumbling a cut-down pistol from a shoulder holster beneath his sheepskin vest. "Stay your hand, friend."

"Stay *this*, ya . . . son of a *bitch*!"

DeRosso didn't get the pistol even half raised before Longarm popped another .44-40 round through his low forehead, just beneath his scalp, throwing the man flat down on his back with an extra spurt of blood from his lips and a raucous fart.

Just as Longarm raised his eyes to the open hall door at the back of the room, a door on the hall's right side opened, and the scrawny, naked visage of Bone McCluskey leaped out in a pink blur, eyes flashing wide in the shadows. There was a shrill scream, and he pulled the pudgy redhead out behind him.

"Longarm, damnit, I just knew they'd send you!"

As he pulled the girl up in front of him, wrapping one hand around her left, jiggling tit, holding her close against him, he stretched a Colt Army with a seven-and-a-half-inch barrel over the girl's pale right shoulder. He squinted one eye and stretched his lips back from his snaggly teeth with a cunning grin.

"Too bad for you, lawdog!"

Longarm lowered his Winchester—he couldn't take a

shot and risk drilling the whore—and dove behind the knocked-askew table and the three dead cardplayers. As he hit the floor, he heard the loud, ringing ping of Bone's gun hammer falling against an empty chamber.

The lawman rolled off his shoulder and came up on a knee left of the table, aiming the rifle straight out from his waist, snarling. In the hall's open doorway, Bone grimaced as he pulled the trigger once more, then bellowed like a wounded griz when the same tinny *clank* filled the room.

He bellowed again as he threw the gun into the main room, bouncing it off a ceiling joist near Longarm. "Gawddamnit!" he raged, giving the pudgy redhead a vicious shove from behind.

As her blunt, creamy shape flew forward, screaming, breasts, belly, and thighs jiggling, curly red hair bouncing around her shoulders, Bone wheeled and, still screaming furiously, ineloquently berating the gods for his empty revolver, bolted off down the hall.

The pudgy redhead fell across one of the dead men and a chair. She went down in a bawling heap while the big woman, having fallen against a cupboard while dodging ricochets, continued bellowing curses over her stout, upraised knees and tented gray dress, her horsey face red as a hot skillet.

Longarm leaped over the whore who was howling down at the bloody dead man beneath her, and bolted to the open hall door. Ahead, the scrawny visage of Bone McCluskey was making for the back door of the place.

"Stop there, Bone, or take one in the back!"

"You wouldn't shoot an unarmed man in the back, Longarm!"

In the dancing shadows, Bone flipped the locking bar from the metal brackets on either side of the door.

"Damn!" Longarm cursed as he lowered the rifle and bolted forward, his low-heeled boots pounding the puncheons.

He wasn't against shooting an unarmed man in the back of his thigh to slow him down or stop him altogether, but it was a long way to Bismarck, and he'd just as soon the man was able to make it there without too much nursemaiding from Longarm.

He was halfway down the hall when Bone, jerking an exasperated look over his bare left shoulder, fumbled the door open and lurched out into the darkness. Longarm heard the man's bare feet smacking the brushy, sandy turf as he gained the open door and looked out.

Starlight glistened off the naked man's scrawny frame as he bounded into the oaks and ash at the base of the hill fifty yards behind the house. Longarm's breath smoked in the frigid air that shoved against him, cold as steel.

He jogged into the yard, past the woodpile and the chopping block. He stopped, raised the rifle, and fired three quick rounds toward the naked man's pale, scissoring feet.

The whip-cracks of the rifle reports rocked the cold, quiet night. One of the slugs spanged off a rock near Bone's left foot. Bone yelped, careened to one side, and ran on. Beneath the Winchester's dying echoes, Longarm could hear the man's raspy, labored breaths, grunts, and groans.

If Bone was like most Western men, north of his boots he was tough as rawhide, able to endure three times the discomfort of your garden-variety city dude. But his feet, accustomed to the protection and cushioning of cotton and leather, were likely tender as a newborn baby's ass. Longarm winced as he listened to the man's dwindling grunts and painful sighs, imagining the burrs and sharp rocks biting into the undersides of the outlaw's tender dogs.

Not only that, but it was damn cold. Ten above or thereabouts. Even a wizened old mountain would die out here within the hour—just curl up under a pine and slip off into the next world.

"Bone, don't be a fool!" Longarm bellowed, his breath visibly billowing around his head. "It's coldern' a banker's heart, old son! You won't make it!"

Longarm started into the brush, still hearing Bone's labored breaths dwindling up the hill through the trees. "That little pecker you love so much is gonna freeze off in the next ten minutes, Bone!"

Silence. Then, in a strained voice muffled with distance: "F-fuck you, L-Longarm!"

Longarm cursed and, lowering the Winchester to his side, started climbing the hill, meandering around the trees. When he was halfway to the crest, he paused beside a sprawling, leafless ash and pricked his ears to listen.

Silence.

Only the occasional scrape of a breeze-brushed branch and the muffled sobs of the whore in the lodge behind him. In the far distance, a lonely wolf loosed a single, forlorn howl.

Longarm cursed again and continued up the grade. When he crested the hill, he stopped and peered into the inky darkness down the other side.

He lifted a gloved hand to the side of his mouth. "Bone, I'm about ten clicks from abandoning your sorry, naked ass to the ravages of the cold Dakota night. You don't have a cat's chance at a dog reunion out here. If the cold doesn't get you in the next half hour, that wolf and his amigos will. Tear you limb from limb."

Longarm chuckled. "But, lookin' on the bright side, you prob'ly won't feel a thing. Why, I bet you're already startin' to numb up." He raised his voice to a mocking pitch. "Are your teeth startin' to chatter yet, Bone? Be careful. The wolves can hear that, and they'll close on you like a duck on a june bug!"

Longarm let a long minute pass, just standing there, boots spread, peering down the other side of the hill, holding his Winchester over his shoulder.

"Well, all righty, then," he said into the silent darkness. "Farewell, Bone. I'm gonna go down and have a cigar and a shot of whiskey. Then maybe I can convince the chief cook and bottle washer to slop me up whatever she's cookin'. Damn, I can smell that good, hot food from here!"

He turned and started back down the hill, adding, "Don't worry—I'll come out and look for ya again in the morning. Probably find ya curled up under a tree, stiff as stone. If the ground's soft enough, I'll dig ya a nice, deep grave!"

He was halfway down the hill when he heard the rasp of labored breath and the pad of bare, running feet behind him. He turned to see a pale figure bound up from the other side of the mountain, faintly silhouetted at the top for a moment before bounding down the grade toward Longarm.

"Hold up, Longarm, damn ya!" Bone jogged, cursing under his breath, toward the grinning lawman. "I reckon I'd rather hang later than freeze to death right now!"

Chapter 3

"Sorta had a feelin' you'd see it my way, Bone," Longarm said, prodding the naked outlaw down the hill in front of him with his Winchester's barrel. "Never did like to cheat the hangman my own self. Nor the undertaker. And in Bismarck, I do believe they're one and the same."

"That's some sense of humor you got there, Longarm." Bone high-stepped it on tender feet toward the lodge's back door through which Longarm could see the sheen of wan lantern light. "Yessir, some real sense of humor. You ever think of joinin' a road show?"

"Nah. I enjoy huntin' rapin', pillagin' killers like yourself too much. And then I like watchin' 'em hang!"

"You just better keep your guard up, ya son of a bitch," Bone said as Longarm prodded him through the lodge's back door. "It's over a hundred miles to Bismarck, and I'm gonna be lookin' to cut your throat every chance I git!"

"Don't doubt it a bit. Stop there, you scrawny devil." Longarm closed the door and, holding his Winchester on the shivering outlaw jogging in place before him and hugging his sparrow chest, stooped to retrieve the locking bar.

"Damnit, I need to git into my duds!" Bone yowled.

"All in good time." Longarm dropped the bar back into place in its bracket and raised the Winchester to his shoulder, aiming at Bone's pale, gaunt face with its misery-racked eyes and blue lips. "I'm gonna let you retrieve your duds from the room in which you were diddlin' that poor redhead, and if you so much as glance at a gun or a knife or any weapon whatsoever"—Longarm lowered the Winchester barrel to Bone's limp, blue dong—"I'm gonna blow that plumb off, ya understand?"

Bone's teeth clattered as he rubbed his arms and hopped from one foot to the other. "I understand! I understand!"

"Go."

Bone wheeled and jogged down the hall. He turned into the room in which he and the redhead were going at it doggy style, and began retrieving his clothes strewn around the bed.

When the outlaw had gathered his clothes in his arms, including his boots and soiled hat, Longarm hazed him back out into the main room. The big, horse-faced woman and the redheaded whore, now dressed in pantaloons and with a blanket draped about her shoulders, had the three dead outlaws lined up side by side on the floor and were going through their clothes. Beside the two dressed cadavers, they'd piled up coins and paper money and rings and even a pair of gold-rimmed eyeglasses.

As Longarm nudged Bone up in front of the fire and ordered the man to dress pronto, the horse-faced woman looked up at the lawman with a sheepish, gap-toothed expression. "You don't mind, do you, lawdog? Figure I gotta right to their truck since you killed 'em on the premises.

Besides, I got at least one bullet hole in every wall and all this damn blood to clean up!"

"Makes sense to me," Longarm said as Bone whipped his longhandles out in front of him, still shaking. "I reckon all the money these fellas stole off stagecoaches and banks an' such is long gone. Ain't that right, Bone?"

Bone chuckled as he quickly stepped into the longhandles. "Blew the last of it in a whorehouse in the river breaks outside Fort Lincoln. I'm so poor that the eagle on my last quarter's dyin' of loneliness."

The horse-faced woman looked up angrily from inspecting the teeth of one of the dead men. "So far, I've tallied four dollars and twenty-six cents and two teeny-weeny little gold fillings. If that's all you fellas got, how in the Sam Hill did you expect to pay for the hooch and cooch you was enjoyin'? I've got the best girls and the best whiskey in the county, and they don't come cheap!"

The woman's shrill, masculine voice resounded around the room. The redheaded whore was prying off one of the dead men's boots, grinding her plump bare feet into the scarred floor puncheons and grunting with the effort. The other girl, who'd been frolicking with Sneaky Pete Whalen, was still on the bed, holding the buffalo robe up to her chin, eyes glazed with shock as she gazed around the blood-splashed room.

Bone had donned his patched buckskin breeches and was pulling on his red flannel shirt, facing the fire and grinning like a dog fox with a mouthful of pullet. "We didn't figure on payin' for it." The scrawny outlaw hiked a shoulder and asked with an arrogant, casual air, "What the hell was you gonna did when we didn't, you fat, ugly bitch?"

A girl's voice said, "Blow your fuckin' oysters off and hear you sing soprano, you limp-dicked son of a bitch!"

The sound of a rifle being cocked in the direction of the open door caused a vein to jump in Longarm's right temple. He swung around, lowering his own carbine from his shoulder.

A slender, tawny-haired girl in men's scruffy trail clothes stood just inside the door, holding a Winchester saddle-ring carbine straight out from her hip. She bore down on Bone McCluskey, her hazel eyes flashing angrily in the firelight.

"Hold on there, little miss," Longarm warned, easing his Winchester into position.

"Cinnamon, goddamnit," the old woman bellowed, "I told you to stay in the barn till I said it was safe to come out."

The girl raked her cool gaze across Longarm and curled her upper lip. "Looks to me like it's safe enough. Who's this big son of a bitch, Ma? Want me to shoot him?"

"He's law," the woman said. "He done blew the wicks on these here brigands. Put that rifle down and go stir my potatoes. Done forgot about 'em in all the excitement, and I can smell 'em burnin'."

The girl held Longarm's inquisitive stare for three long beats, then dropped her eyes, faintly challenging now, to the lawman's Winchester. She depressed the hammer on her own carbine, lowered it, and raked her eyes quickly up and down Longarm's tall, broad-shouldered frame. Her tanned, perfectly sculpted cheeks colored slightly.

Wheeling, causing her brush-scarred bat-wing chaps to flutter about her well-turned legs, she kicked the door closed, leaned her rifle against a cupboard, and headed for the smoking pan atop the range.

As she did, Longarm couldn't help staring at her back. Her black denims were drawn tight across her firm, round butt and the faintly rounded hips of a girl just entering her prime.

"Get your eyes off my daughter, damn ya!" bellowed the horse-faced woman, raking her angry, gray eyes between Longarm and Bone, both of whom, the lawman realized suddenly, were gawking hang-jawed at the spry little vixen with long, tawny hair and in bat-wing chaps. "She tends the stables and the stables only. Cinnamon is strictly off-limits to males of any stripe, lawdogs and four flushin' killers included!"

"Jesus H. Christ!" Bone exclaimed, dropping his jaw even farther and gesturing at Cinnamon stirring the potatoes at the range, her back to the room. "You mean you was hidin' *that* in the stables? Why, you sneaky old *hag*!"

Cinnamon cast a quick, coy look over her shoulder, then went back to the sizzling potatoes.

The woman gritted her teeth and reached for one of the dead men's blood-splattered pistols. "Who're you callin' a hag, you peckerwood?"

"All right, all right," Longarm castigated, stomping across the room and jerking the Remy from the woman's hands before she could get the hammer locked back. "I'd like to take at least one of these peckerwoods back to Bismarck. It ain't only the public callin' for a hangin', but nearly every federal badge toter west of St. Louis and north of the Rio Bravo. They got one hell of a necktie party planned down by the river docks in Bismarck, and I'd hate like hell to ride in without one of the five sittin' upright and rain on the whole parade, so to speak."

He kicked a couple of other pistols against a wall and stuffed the Remy behind his cartridge belt as he swung back toward Bone, who was now stomping into his boots and assaulting the horse-faced woman with an evil leer. Longarm whipped a set of nickel-plated handcuffs from his coat pocket and tossed them at the outlaw, who caught the cuffs with a startled grunt.

"Put them on, Bone. Lock 'em up tight. Good an' tight, or I'll do it myself." Longarm turned to the woman. "You got somewhere snug I can bed him down for the night, maybe chain him up?"

Longarm had been tracking the killers for weeks with no more than three hours of shut-eye at a time. He'd like to have Bone safely put away for the night, somewhere Longarm wouldn't have to worry about the scrawny owl-hoot getting away and getting his hands on a horse or gun or both, so the lawman could pamper himself with a long, badly needed snooze.

He was still facing a good clip back to Bismarck, after all.

The old woman twirled a gilded spur on a black boot. "Birthing stall in the barn'll do." She cast a hateful glance at the prisoner who was bent over, attaching the cuffs to his wrists. "Lock him up good if you want him dancing in midair in Bismarck, Marshal. I got my girls and my innocent daughter to protect . . . and I'll be sleepin' with a double-barreled shotgun tonight. And believe me when I tell you I know how to use it . . . and ain't afeared to use it, neither!"

Cinnamon cast another look over her shoulder at Longarm, her faintly provocative eyes causing Longarm to wonder just how innocent she was.

Longarm wagged his Winchester barrel at the door. "Chop-chop, Bone. The birthing stall, it is."

"I'll show ya." Cinnamon slid the pan of potatoes to one side of the hot stove lid and grabbed a lantern off a shelf.

"You'll do no such thing, young lady!"

"Oh, hush, Ma," Cinnamon retorted with a weary, defiant air as she headed for the door. "The marshal's done got his prisoner all trussed up like a hog fer the slaughter. He don't know where the birthing stall is, and I'm gonna show him."

With that, she opened the door and went out into the night with the horse-faced woman snarling curses behind her as she continued going through the dead man's plunder with a growing air of frustration.

Bone chuckled as Longarm prodded him out the door and into the cold night air and the darkness of the barnyard. "I like how she walks in them tight denim breeches, don't you?" the outlaw said.

Longarm had to admit the girl cut a fine figure, and her round bottom and long legs clad in those leather chaps were improving the blood flow to his loins, which had been restricted by all the time he'd spent in the saddle lately. But he said, "Shut up, Bone. Figured you had enough for one night."

"A man like me, Longarm, can never get enough."

They moved around a springhouse roofed in corrugated tin and approached the stout log barn sitting kitty-corner across the yard from the house and abutted on one side with a lean-to shed and a corral. Weeds and shrubs grew up around the barn, which was roofed in dead sod, but the yard fronting the place was pancake flat and frozen hard as sheet iron.

Beside a low, timbered door next to the two larger main doors, the girl fumbled with the lantern, rattling the chimney. Finally she struck a match on her chaps, lit the lantern's wick, and closed the chimney with a raspy screech. The old bull's-eye lantern glowed redly in front of her, silhouetting her slender, round-hipped figure before it as she opened the door and ducked inside.

"A roll in the hay on a cold night," Bone said, chuckling once more and stopping dead in his tracks to lift his chin toward the starry sky. "Just what the doctor ordered!"

Longarm rammed the rifle barrel between the killer's shoulder blades, shoving him forward.

"Oh, mercy!" Bone stumbled forward against the right-side door frame.

The outlaw wheeled suddenly and, with a low snarl and in a shadowy blur of motion, bolted back toward Longarm. He raised his shackled wrists, and the cuffs flashed in the starlight.

Longarm, who hadn't been born yesterday or even the day before, had seen Bone's escape attempt telegraphed in the set of the man's shoulder. The lawman took one fluid step straight back, whipped the Winchester out to one side, then smashed it hard against Bone's left temple.

"Oh!" Bone dropped his cuffed hands, staggered back against the door frame, and began to sag as his knees buckled. "Oh . . . oh, Jesus!"

Longarm lurched forward and, taking his rifle in one hand, grabbed Bone's shirt collar with his free hand, holding the man upright while wedging him against the barn with one knee.

Before him, Cinnamon poked her head out the barn door, frowning, her cinnamon hair glistening alluringly in the lantern's umber glow. "What happened?"

"Poor man's so dang tired, he couldn't even make it to bed."

Cinnamon drew back away from the door, and Longarm sort of dragged, carried, and kicked the unconscious outlaw through it and into the barn.

Chapter 4

"How many men you killed, Marshal?" Cinnamon's eyes sparked in the lantern light as she ran her gaze up and down Longarm's tall frame for the sixth or seventh time in the past half hour. "I mean . . . if you don't mind me askin'?"

Longarm snorted and dropped his gaze into the hay-strewn birthing stall in which Bone McCluskey lay curled up on one side beneath a couple of heavy saddle blankets and a buffalo robe. The lawman had wrapped a logging chain around the outlaw's waist and one ankle, then attached it to a stout metal ring deeply embedded in a solid plank wall. He'd secured the chain with a rusty but workable padlock the size of a big man's fist.

Even if Longarm hadn't cracked the man's skull with the barrel of his Winchester, laying him out cold, Bone McCluskey wouldn't be going anywhere until Longarm made it possible.

As Bone snored like a rusty saw cutting corrugated tin, Longarm said with a casual, bemused air, "Hell, I don't mind. Problem is, I killed so damn many I lost count about five, six years ago now. Used to keep track on my cartridge belt—you know, with notches an' all—but I either got bored with all that or just plain ran out of room!"

The girl's cheeks flushed in the lantern light, and her bosom heaved slightly.

Chuckling to himself, Longarm looked around. "I'll sleep out here, keep an eye on my prisoner." As he headed for the door he said to the girl, "I'm gonna fetch my horse. Tell your ma I'd appreciate some vittles. I'll pay her for 'em. Then I believe I'll bed down in the hay. Got a long ride ahead."

"You can sleep in the lean-to," the girl said quickly, hooking a thumb over her shoulder. "That's where I sleep sometimes, to get away from the racket inside, if ya catch my drift. I build a fire in the stove."

Longarm tipped his hat to the girl and went out.

When Longarm had fetched his horse from the ridge behind the brothel, he stabled the mount in the barn that Bone McCluskey was nearly tearing down with his raucous snores. The dead men's horses were there, snorting and munching hay in the aromatic shadows, occasionally knocking a stall partition with a start when Bone's snores and sighs rose abruptly.

The lawman unleathered his own beast, rubbed him down good, and threw a blanket over his back to keep him warm through the long Dakota night.

Then he returned to the cabin for a quick meal, which Cinnamon, acting sort of coy and shy and flirtatious all at the same time, dished up herself, hovering nearby to keep Longarm's coffee cup full and even offering a second helping of antelope steak and fried potatoes.

"Ah, nah," Longarm said, sliding back his chair and scrubbing his mouth with his napkin. "I could probably hold a little more, but then I wouldn't sleep on it. I'm much obliged, Miss Cinnamon."

"No trouble," the girl said, hiking a shoulder noncommittally as she carried the pan back to the stove.

Her horse-faced ma, whose name Longarm had learned was Miss Eunice, and the two whores had straightened up the room and dragged the bodies out to the woodshed. There were still a couple of stubborn bloodstains on the floor, but they'd fade in time. Longarm would leave Miss Eunice a couple of dollars, which he'd record on his government travel voucher, for trouble and damages as well as for food and board.

Miss Eunice sat in the big bed beyond the woodstove now, barely visible in the cabin's dim, smoky light, drinking whiskey from a water glass while darning a wool sock. She seemed worn out and owly, and Longarm had a feeling it was her customary temperament aggravated by the fact that she'd taken so little bounty from the four stiffs now awaiting burial in the woodshed.

"I believe I'll be turning in." Longarm tipped his hat to Miss Eunice and reached for his coat hanging from a wall hook. "Much obliged for the hospitality, ma'am."

"Ain't like I invited ya," the woman groused, looking up briefly from her work. "Next time you turn my place into a turkey shoot, make sure the brigands you bring down got a little jingle on 'em."

"You can keep the horses," Longarm told her, buttoning his coat and reaching for the door handle.

Miss Eunice only grunted.

"Will you be wantin' breakfast before you head out in the mornin', Marshal?" Cinnamon asked. She'd sat down at the table and was rolling a quirley from a makings pouch, looking up at Longarm from beneath her thin, cinnamon brows.

She had almond-shaped, blue green eyes, high cheekbones, and a sharp nose. A damn pretty girl with the smell of the earth on her, not to mention a pair of good-sized breasts pushing out her striped, collarless shirt and deerskin vest.

Miss Eunice cleared her throat in admonishment and said, "Quit starin' at my daughter's tits, Marshal. I know it's a cold, dark night, and you've ridden far, but if you wanna spend the night between a pair of warm thighs, that'll be five dollars and you can head upstairs to Dory or Kansas City Jane. They're practiced in the arts of man pleasin'. Cinnamon here is bein' saved for marriage to a well-heeled son of a bitch preferably from somewhere back East!"

Longarm's face warmed as Cinnamon stared up at him, smiling lustily as she scratched a lucifer to life on the rim of his coffee cup. She fired her quirley, blowing smoke out around it and snuffing the match.

Grinning with embarrassment, his loins swelling, Longarm donned his hat and hurried outside. He strode quickly across the yard toward the barn, drawing deep draughts of the bone-splintering night air and lifting his scarf for another sniff of the distinctive scent of Cynthia Larimer. He thought the smell would quell the nettling lust pangs evoked by the sexy, earthy Cinnamon, but it only made his loins throb harder.

Drawing another deep lungful of cold air and turning his thoughts to the long trail facing him tomorrow, he shoved the small barn door open with a raspy wooden rake and a squawk of rusty hinges. He paused just inside the threshold, the brittle air pushing in around him, listening.

The hair on the back of his neck pricked with apprehension when he was greeted by only the snorts and soft thuds of the horses concealed by the barn's heavy shadows.

Had Bone McCluskey woken up from his stupor and somehow worked himself free of the log chain?

Longarm's right hand began moving toward the double-action Frontier-model Colt positioned for the cross draw on his left hip. He stayed the hand when, suddenly from the deep silence and aromatic darkness, a long, raucous snore rose from the birthing stall ahead and left. The din rose to a near-shrill pitch, stopped dead for two full seconds, then rose again as the killer let the air trickle back out of his scrawny chest, making a sound like pent-up steam expunged from a suddenly opened escape valve.

Longarm closed the barn door and, forgoing a lantern, gathered his bedroll, war bag, and rifle, then felt his way to the door to the little lean-to addition in which Cinnamon had laid a fire.

It was a nice, neat little room with a few sticks of crude furniture and a large bed that, piled as it was with hides and quilts and big pillows, was obviously in frequent use.

Cinnamon's own private hideaway.

Just as he could smell Cynthia Larimer's perfume on his scarf, he thought he detected a faint cherry musk that was likely Cinnamon's own singular, feminine aroma.

He remembered the girl grilling him on how many men he'd killed, and he gave a snort as he shrugged out of his coat and hung it on the antler rack beside the door. A foxy little vixen, Cinnamon. Longarm found the delicate, cultured Cynthia Larimer about as rapturous as anything he could think of, but he'd found tomboys—especially tomboys who looked good in a pair of brush-scarred leather chaps and a work shirt—uniquely enticing and wildly satisfying under the sheets.

Too bad the girl had a mother who guarded her purity as though it were the cremated remains of a treasured relative gathering dust on the fireplace mantel.

The fire in the sheet-iron woodstove had burned down to an umber glow, but soon after Longarm had added a few split oak logs, the room was comfortably warm, the stove ticking and sighing while the cool breeze howled beneath the outside eaves.

The lawman stripped down to his longhandles, took note of a thunder mug peeking out from beneath a small table—he might need that later—then washed in a porcelain basin filled with fresh, albeit bracingly cold, water.

The girl had thought of everything.

When he'd washed and stretched and sat down on the edge of the bed, he took a couple of nips from his bottle of Maryland rye, noting that he had only an inch left—only an inch to get him through the long, cold miles back to Bismarck!—then stuck the bottle back in his war bag, and crawled under heavy, musty, but comfortable hides and quilts. Bone McCluskey's long, shrill snores continued from the birthing stall. Feeling his muscles and his mind slowly relax, the hard kinks unknotting, Longarm let his head sag back against a soft, deep feather pillow.

He sighed. Right nice furnishings for this backside of frozen nowhere.

He didn't know how long he'd been asleep when a sound woke him. A sound other than McCluskey's snores, which continued with the regular beats of a metronome. One of the horses kicked its stall with a start, and then the door latch clicked just a few feet away from the end of Longarm's bed.

The lawman reached for the .44-40 jutting from the holster that he'd hung on a front bedpost and rocked the hammer back. The ratcheting scrape sounded loud in the quiet room lit by only a pulsating brickred glow around the stove's warped door.

Over the gun barrel he watched as well as heard the door open and a bulky, furry figure steal into the room. For a moment Longarm thought he was being visited by a small bruin trying to escape the penetrating plains chill.

Then the figure stepped toward the stove, and the brickred glow glistened like copper in Cinnamon's lustrous tawny hair, which tumbled down over the broad collar of her long, black bear coat.

The girl stood between the stove and the bed, reeking of the slightly gamey odor of the coat and the cold-steel smell of the chill night air. She gave both feet a kick, and her high-topped fur boots skidded and rolled toward the bed.

"Whoa, now," Longarm said, depressing his Colt's hammer with another ratcheting click. "I don't remember ringin' for room service."

The girl gave a lusty, throaty chuckle, and then she slid the coat off her shoulders, letting it drop straight down around her ankles. Her long, creamy legs and high breasts shone in the dim firelight as she strode toward him, lifting her hands and pushing the firm, lovely orbs together, her hair flopping loosely about her oval face and tumbling down her shoulders.

Longarm's tongue was damn near literally tied in a knot in the dead center of his throat as the girl dropped to a knee at the edge of the bed and wrapped her hand around the Colt hanging limp in his right hand. She pulled the gun away and dropped it back down in its holster with a leather snick.

"The stories I bet that gun could tell," Cinnamon said, breathing hard as she lifted the hides and quilts and slid down close beside Longarm. "But I bet you got another one that could tell just as many!"

With that she walked her fingers down his chest and across his belly, and he sucked a sharp breath as she wrapped her cold, smooth, long-fingered hand around his already throbbing cock.

"Whoa, now," he repeated, softer this time. Actually, it was more of a croak.

Before he could continue, Cinnamon said, "I know—you don't remember ringin' for room service." She pressed her lips to his broad chest and drew a deep breath, sucking his smell deep into her lungs. "But I remember you ringin' that bell plain as day."

Her hand dropped down the hard length of his cock to cup his balls, then drift up his shaft once more, flooding his body with hot male urgency that dimmed his mind like several large shots of stout busthead, but which only stoked the sudden wildfire in his nether regions.

She coiled her right leg around his left leg as she kissed her way down his chest and belly, her silky hair sliding along behind her moist, full lips that left hot, moist spots on his skin in their backtrail.

He could feel the tender rake of her breasts and jutting nipples down his belly, and then the orbs were hugging his cock in their silky-warm cocoon for two or three sweet seconds before her mouth dropped over the head and suddenly he was in her throat with her tongue tangled around him as she sucked, groaning and humping his leg like an amorous dog and reaching up to knead his chest almost painfully.

"Jesus . . . H. Christ!" he gasped, stretching his lips back from his teeth and pressing his head far back against the pillow. "Somethin' tells me . . . Miss Cinnamon . . . you . . . ain't . . . nowhere's near as . . . pure as . . . your sweet ma . . . *says*!"

The girl choked out a laugh as she continued raising and lowering her head, her wet lips moving fluidly up and down his shaft that was so hard by now he thought the skin would split like that of an overcooked sausage. At the same time, Cinnamon used one hand to pump him, her mouth and hand working in such a fine rhythm that Longarm sailed off into the sweet carnal ecstasy known by only those men in the care of a woman proficient in the delicate and hard-learned art of fellatio.

If he died now—if Bone McCluskey was to suddenly work himself free, lay his hands on a gun, and burst into the room suddenly, gun blazing, Longarm would not only not be able to defend himself, he wouldn't want to.

There was neither life nor death, neither well-being nor pain. There was only the misty, ecstatic, intoxicating, all-encompassing netherworld of fulfilled lust and desire that is the closest any man will ever get to rapture on earth or, most likely, anywhere else.

Cinnamon brought him to the edge of climax, held him there for one long, blistering, sweet minute, at once nibbling, sucking, and kissing the very end of his swollen dong. Then, just as he was about to explode, curling his toes and clutching at the bedding with his fists, she slid her mouth down onto him once more, sucking hard, and his boiling seed fired like the rounds of a Gatling gun down her expanding and contracting throat.

"Jesus H. Christ!" she said, gagging as she slid her mouth off his cock and wiped her mouth and nose with the back of her hand. "What're you tryin' to do—*kill* me?"

"I was just about to ask you the same thing," Longarm said, feeling as though he'd just had the wind knocked out of him.

He sucked a deep breath as the girl lay her head on his chest, snuggling her warm, slightly swollen love nest atop his dwindling cock and running her hands across his broad shoulders, down his thick arms, and back up to his stout neck. Her body fairly radiated desire.

"I take it dear Mom don't know what she's got on her hands," he said, running his hands through the girl's hair, his chest rising and falling heavily.

Cinnamon giggled and wriggled around again on his member. The organ had been so violently abused that he was surprised that the girl's movements actually caused another spark down there, which was likely her intent.

"I wasn't born with my . . . um . . . talents," she said, groaning and sighing like a cat as she continued to wriggle around and run her hands around on him. "Momma thinks she's savin' me for some rich Easterner. Pshaw! Where's she gonna find a rich Easterner out here? They don't fall out of the trees like apples. In the meantime, a girl's got desires."

Longarm cupped the girl's firm, round ass in his hands—they nearly covered each entire cheek—and drew her nest down tighter against his improbably reawakening member. "Yeah, I reckon she does."

"A big Indian—a full-blooded Lakota Sioux—taught me how to suck like that. We started when I was only fourteen, but just last year, Momma caught us out in the woodshed together. We were only kissing—right then, anyways—and she went after him with a sickle. Haven't seen him since, but I'm glad I haven't lost my touch."

"Me, too."

The girl rose up on Longarm's chest and closed her mouth over his—a hard, hot kiss. She pulled away and regarded him sidelong, her pretty, skeptical eyes crossing slightly. "You really kill as many men as you said you did?"

Longarm squinted one eye. "I might have stretched it by one or two, but only one or two."

"Damn! That just makes me hornier than a she-griz with the springtime craze!" Cinnamon reached down between her legs and grabbed his dong, engorged once more.

Her eyes sparked, and the corners of her mouth rose with devilish delight. "Come on," she said, rising to her hands and knees then spinning around to face the foot of the bed, her exquisite bottom facing him, the smooth skin glowing burnt orange in the firelight.

Longarm rose to his elbows, blinking against a lock of brown hair in his eye. "Miss Cinnamon, I don't relish the idea of your momma comin' after me with a sickle." He glanced at his throbbing member saluting the rafters. "Especially in my vulnerable state!"

"Momma drank a whole bottle of hooch and passed out two hours ago. She makes Mr. McCluskey's snores sound like the purrs of a newborn kitten."

Cinnamon laughed, wagged her ass, and glanced at Longarm over her shoulder, throwing her long hair across her back. "Let's do it doggy style!"

Chapter 5

"Damnit, Longarm—I'm so cold I think my pecker's done froze to my thigh," Bone McCluskey complained late the next afternoon, when he and Longarm were wending their way across the rolling, dun brown prairie south of the whorehouse.

They'd gotten a late start because Longarm had taken the time to bury the four dead outlaws in a single, shallow grave after thawing the nearly frozen earth with a bonfire. Now the sun was falling into the western hogbacks, painting the few high, thin clouds all the colors on a painter's palette.

A breeze stirred, sharp as a knife blade against Longarm's cheeks.

In the far southern distance he spied the slinking stroll of a wolf moving along the crest of brushy hillock before disappearing down the other side. It was the third wolf he'd seen that day.

"Shut up back there, Bone," he growled as his rented pinto hoofed it down a short, steep rise. "Done had enough of your complainin'. In fact, tomorrow I believe that in addition to tying you to your saddle, I'll muzzle you, as well.

Make the rest of the trip back to Bismarck a whole lot more peaceable."

"Oh, yeah? You think so? I got rights, you son of a bitch, and bein' muzzled so I can't complain about your ill treatment of me ain't one of 'em."

"Yessir, that's exactly what I'm gonna do." Longarm reined up at the bottom of the rise, using the lead rope to draw Bone's claybank up alongside him. "I'm gonna muzzle you up tighter than a drumhead."

"What're you lookin' at?" the prisoner asked.

"That creek yonder." Longarm stared across the quickly darkening hogbacks brushed with a stiffening breeze toward a line of leafless, spidery trees following the base of a low ridge about a mile away. "Good cover in there. Wood for a fire. We'll stop there for the night, so quit your damn complainin'."

Bone turned to Longarm, his wind-burned cheeks scrunched with anger. "That's two miles away! Hell, my dick'll be hard as stone by the time we reach that creek. Why can't we hole up right here, between these two hills?"

"You see any firewood?"

Bone had a quick look around, his cuffed hands secured with rope to his saddle horn. "I see cow pies. Plenty of 'em. And if we need wood, you can ride out to the creek and gather some later." The outlaw, try as he might to maintain a sober expression, cracked a guilty grin.

"You'd like that, wouldn't ya?" Longarm gave a wry chuff. "You'd just love for me to leave you alone so you could figure a way out of your current dilemma."

"Or so a wolf could git ya," Bone said, his eyes flashing eagerly. "Or maybe a griz. They hunt at night, too, don't they?"

"Like I said. Gonna find me a muzzle . . ."

Longarm clucked to his horse and, pulling Bone's claybank along behind him, headed for the creek, gritting his teeth as the breeze picked up, the icy night chill slipping under his collar and down his neck. Bone was right. A fire was going to feel good. What would feel even better was Miss Cinnamon in his bedroll tonight, but the voluptuous little wolverine was a good twenty-five miles north, back again under the watchful eye of her horse-faced ma.

Longarm would have to settle for the aroma of Miss Cynthia Larimer, which he could still sniff in his scarf from time to time if he took a deep enough breath . . .

Twenty minutes later, he pulled the horses into the trees, the only grove of any size that he could see for miles. Out here, there were mainly just a few cottonwoods or elms growing on the lee sides of hillocks or swales, where water collected.

The sun was all but down, just a little green light lingering. The breeze-swept prairie was cloaked in ever-deepening shadows. Several stars kindled in the east, and a lone wolf started howling, the mournful wail swirling on the breeze so that it was hard to get a fix on the beast. It was also hard to tell how far away it was. At least a mile. If it was any closer, the lawman hoped it had a full belly or an aversion to humans.

He'd be picketing the horses close to the camp tonight. The pinto and the claybank would keep their ears and nose pricked for any such prairie predators all night long.

Longarm stepped down from his saddle, wincing at his cold-stiffened muscles, and tied the pinto to a cottonwood branch.

"Sure hope you got a bottle," Bone said as Longarm

cut the prisoner's right boot free of the stirrup. "I need a drink powerful bad."

"Might be able to scrounge one up."

Bone chuckled as Longarm walked around to cut the other boot free of its stirrup. "Damn, Longarm—you're all right. You know that?"

"Been called many things," Longarm said, reaching up to free the man's cuffed hands from the saddle horn. " 'All right'—now, that's a new one." He clipped a yawn as he closed his pocketknife and stepped back away from Bone's claybank.

"What's the matter, lawdog?" Bone said, grinning. "Didn't get enough sleep last night?"

Longarm slipped his double-action Colt Frontier from its holster and frowned up at Bone, incredulous.

The scrawny, patch-bearded outlaw spread his plump cheeks away from his big teeth. "That Miss Cinnamon, she sure can rock the rafters . . . when a fella's throwin' the blocks to her, that is. Yessir, I woke up in the middle of the damn night, and I thought a griz had broke into the cabin and was attackin' the women, eatin' 'em all up real slow-like. Then I heard above the ringin' in my ears from the unwarranted brainin' you gave me, this awful, blood-curdlin' squealin' and screamin' and groanin' comin' *not* from the cabin but from the very *barn* I was sleepin' in!"

Bone laughed. "You musta been floggin' that girl awful hard, Longarm!"

"Cimb on down from there and don't make any sudden moves. You're right, I'm tired and I ain't in the mood for any more of your bullshit."

Bone grabbed the saddle horn and swung his right boot over the claybank's butt. When he was on the ground, he looked up at Longarm, who had a good three inches on the scruffy, diminutive outlaw, and grinned his insolent grin. "Tell me—was I just dreamin', or did I hear you throwin' the blocks to that sweet little Cinnamon last night in the barn's side room?"

Longarm felt the tips of his ears warm in spite of the cold wind. "You were dreamin'." He rummaged around in his saddlebags for a set of leg irons, then brusquely turned the outlaw around by his shoulder and shoved him toward a little clearing in the trees, where the grass had been mashed flat by several deer or elk.

Bone chuckled mockingly. "I sure thought it was her I heard screamin'. Maybe it was just my own head screamin' out in misery from that brainin' you give me . . . and which, by the way, I'll be talkin' to a lawyer about. You can count on that."

"I'll be countin'," Longarm growled as he followed the outlaw into the trees.

The lawman shoved the outlaw down against a broad cottonwood bole. Bone grinned up at him, the wind buffeting his raised coat collar. "Nah, now I think about it—I'm just certain sure it was that sassy Cinnamon girl I heard screamin' like she was gettin' it with a brandin' iron. Tell me, was she any good?"

"Stow it, Bone," Longarm said with a weary sigh as he closed a shackle around the outlaw's right ankle. When he'd locked the other shackle around the man's other ankle, he said with a liberal dose of threat in his voice, "Now I'm gonna build a fire and put coffee on. You rest easy and keep your mouth shut, and, if you're good, when I'm done with my chores I'll pour you out a nice long shot of busthead." He gave a schoolmaster's dry wink. "But only if you're good. And that means keepin' your mouth shut."

Bone just scowled up at him, lips pursed.

Longarm straightened, keeping his admonishing eyes on the outlaw, then turned away and strode off toward the horses.

"I'm just sayin' it ain't fair—that's all," Bone groused behind him, his voice pitched with exasperation. "That ugly old trollop hidin' the good one away and then you come in, kill all my boys, and run me off bare-assed naked in the cold night—and a few minutes later you're bonin' the purtiest little piece o' . . ."

Bone let his voice trail off as Longarm turned to admonish him with a warning look.

"Ah, never mind," Bone said, dropping his gaze like a chastised schoolboy, grinding his heels into the hard, cold ground.

Longarm turned and continued over to where the horses stood cropping the spindly wheatgrass. He had both mounts unleathered and tied to a short picket line in ten minutes. Ten minutes after that, he'd rubbed both beasts down with handfuls of dry grass and draped feed sacks of oats over their ears.

When he'd hauled his and Bone's tack over to the clearing, he used his folding shovel to dig out a fire pit. He ringed the pit with rocks, then, glad to see the outlaw silently dozing, hunkered down low against the tree, hands shoved down between his drawn-up knees, Longarm headed off in search of dry wood for a fire.

When he had enough wood to last the night—a pile about three feet high and twice as wide and long—he put coffee on to boil and then rigged up a couple of green willow twigs with which he'd roast the venison haunch he'd bought from the horse-faced Miss Eunice. Bone was so cold now that his thoughts seemed more on rest and warmth than on how he'd missed out on the talents of the lovely Miss Cinnamon—talents that Longarm, for his part, couldn't help mulling, half wondering if he hadn't dreamt the whole beguiling encounter.

Finding a lovely girl as talented as Miss Cinnamon in the middle of frozen nowhere was one fine piece of luck. It was just him and Bone tonight, however. And what little scent of Cynthia remained in his scarf. As he skewered the heavy venison haunch and held it out over a corner of the crackling fire, the heat pressing against him and just now starting to wrestle some of the cold from his bones, he glanced at the dozing outlaw once more.

He gave a mirthless chuff. The sleeping conditions would be far, far different tonight from last night.

The outlaw kicked around angrily and lifted his head. "Damnit, Longarm. Throw some more wood on the fire, would ya? It's damn cold out here. Don't see why you couldn't have waited till spring to track us down."

"To be right honest with ya, Bone," Longarm said, turning the skewered meat, "I don't, either. I'll add more wood when the meat's done, unless you want yours burned black as your outlaw heart.

"Very fuckin' funny. That coffee done yet?"

"In a bit. You want any of it . . ."

"I know, I know. Shut up."

"Damn, Bone," Longarm said. "By the time we get to Bismarck, you and me might just be tighter'n long-lost pards."

Bone spat out one side of his mouth as he hunkered deeper into his coat, his hat tipped low over his forehead. "Wouldn't count on it."

"Me, neither."

When the coffee was chugging up a racket, Longarm

propped the skewers on rocks, then poured him and Bone a cup of the scalding belly wash, adding a liberal jigger of the cheap whiskey that he'd also purchased from the horse-faced madam. They were both about half finished with their coffee when the meat was done, and they ate across the fire from each other, hungrily chewing the tough but flavorful meat in silence, washing down their sizable mouthfuls with the steaming, well-laced coffee.

The food and coffee served to help fight the chill out of Longarm's bones. It also made him sleepy. After he'd checked on the horses once more, removing their feed bags, he walked down by the frozen creek to look around and listen and to evacuate his bladder onto the rocks lining the stream. The stars were bright and clear in the cold-scoured sky, obscured by only the billowing vapor of his breaths as he watched them.

Back at the bivouac, Bone was already curled up in his blanket roll, snoring nearly as loudly as he'd been snoring last night when Longarm and Cinnamon had been copulating like rabid wolverines.

Longarm tossed more wood on the fire, building a good blaze, then tugged his boots off and, keeping his mackinaw on, as it would likely get down to near zero tonight and he'd need all the insulation he could get, he rolled up in his own blankets, resting his head on his saddle and tipping his hat over his eyes.

He pulled up the scarf, giving it a good sniff. Smiling, he slept.

He woke a couple of hours later to build up the fire. An hour or so after that, one of the horses nickered, and he jerked out of his traditional light slumber, automatically grabbing his .44 from its oiled holster coiled beside him, and rocking back the hammer. He stared into the dense night shadows stitched with light, swirling snowflakes.

On the other side of the fire, Bone was snoring, whistling.

A rustling sounded from the creek. The taps of light, padded feed. A snort.

On the other side of the fire, Bone grunted, smacked his lips, and continued snoring.

Longarm tossed his covers aside, pulled his boots on. He slowly gained his feet, looking around cautiously, revolver extended, then grabbed a burning log from the fire. Holding the torch up high in his free hand, he moved slowly through the dark trees, his boots crunching the half inch of light, granular snow that had fallen from the starless sky. The cold slid around him, and he shivered in spite of the heat shed by the burning branch in his hand.

As he approached the frozen creek, several sets of small copper eyes shone ahead and left, jostling around in the darkness. There was a low, eerie mewling and another soft snort.

Longarm hurled the torch toward the copper eyes, lighting for an instant several shaggy wolves as they wheeled and, yipping and moaning softly, scrambled off through the trees on the other side of the rocky stream. As the torch died in the snow, the wolves thudded and crunched through the brush, the sounds quickly dwindling as the predators fled over the top of the bank and headed off across the prairie.

Longarm gave a wry snort of his own. The wolves were no real threat. There was plenty of game around. They were just curious. Shivering, the big lawman headed back to the fire, upon which he tossed a few more logs, building the flames high, then rolled up in his blankets once more, turned onto his side, and drifted quickly back to sleep.

A shrill whinny cut deep into a dirty dream he was having about frolicking with both Cynthia Larimer and Cinnamon at the same time. Longarm jerked his head up again, knocking his hat off his forehead, and reached for his Colt as the answering whinny of another horse rose in the distance.

He stared northward.

The blue light of early dawn lay lightly over the dun prairie grass dusted with sugary snow. The snow had stopped falling, and a few pale stars shone through the high, thin clouds. A hundred yards from the camp, three horseback riders rose up from the far side of a low hogback. It was hard to see in the misty light, but two appeared to hold rifles across their saddle pommels. A third held his own rifle straight up from his thigh.

All three wore heavy coats and Stetson hats tied to their heads with scarves.

Longarm rose slowly, frowning and watching the riders disappear into another crease in the prairie as they came on toward the camp.

"Now, what the hell do you fellas want?" he muttered, reaching for his hat.

Chapter 6

The three riders climbed up out of another trough and approached the camp within fifty yards now and closing, the thuds of their horses' shod hooves sounding clear on the still, cold air. Longarm holstered his .44—no point in sparking trouble where none was intended—as he inspected the three hombres. It was hard to tell in this light, but they appeared to be one older man and two young ones, all in heavy coats and scarves.

Likely three stockmen merely riding in to inquire about his presence. Maybe they thought he was inspecting the environs with the intention of filing his own claim—something established ranchers, with large herds to feed, didn't smile on.

Longarm must have blended well with the trees around him, because the three came on at a fast trot and were pulling up within ten yards when the older, slope-shouldered gent on the left, wearing a heavy, quilted leather mackinaw and shabby Stetson, snapped his eyes wide and jerked back on the reins of his skewbald paint.

"Whoa!" he said, frowning, as his horse lurched back.

The two younger gents saw Longarm at nearly the same

time, and they halted their own mounts just as suddenly, the buckskin on the far right giving a startled whinny. One of Longarm's horses answered the whinny from back in the trees, and when the horses' conversation was over, the lawman fashioned a taut smile and said, "Howdy there, gents. What can I do ya for?"

The older man—mid-fifties, with a round, moonlike face, thin patch beard, and large blue eyes—held his reins taut against his chest with one hand while keeping his grip on his old Spencer rifle with the other. Longarm sensed the man's edginess, as well as that of the two younger men before him—one long-haired, hawk-faced, and in his twenties, the other stocky and younger and with a heavy brow.

"You that lawman?"

"What lawman might that be?" Longarm said, crossing his arms on his chest and spreading his feet. He didn't like the newcomer's challenging tone.

"The one Kansas City Jane told us about back at Sand Creek." The older gent jerked his head to indicate his backtrail. "The one cleaned the clocks of Sneaky Pete Whalen, Bryce Coyle, and the weird-looking fella, DeRosso."

"You mean to tell me you followed me all the way out here from Sand Creek?"

"Sure as shit up a cow's ass, we did." The youngest of the trio had a deep, belligerent voice to go with his round, belligerent face that resembled the older gent's enough to make him a son. The other didn't look much like the older man, but Longarm figured he was the man's offspring as well.

The older boy rose up in his saddle and leaned this way and that, trying to get a look into the trees behind Longarm. "Is that McCluskey over there by the fire?"

Longarm hooded his eyes. His tone was skeptical, wary. "It is."

"We want him," the old man said bluntly, nostrils flaring as he stared hard at Longarm over his paint's head. "We want him now, and I'll brook no argument. The man savaged my daughter, put her in the family way last time that evil foursome ran roughshod through the county. Stopped at my ranch when me and my boys were out workin' the herd, dragged my youngest girl off, and put a bun in her oven. Girl's pret' near big as a house and owly as hell, and I'm stringin' up that savage. Gonna play cat's cradle with his head. Stretch his neck a good three feet, I swear!"

"Yessir," the older kid intoned, nodding. "He done violated our sister, blackened her soul so the Lord ain't hardly gonna recognize her, and for that he's gotta *dangle*!"

Bone McCluskey's voice rose behind Longarm. "Weren't no savage about it, ya crazy sons o' bitches! Wanda came as willin' as a newborn goat to the milk bottle! Hell, she's had eyes fer me ever since I worked at the Jamieson place!"

"Bone McCluskey!" the old man roared, sitting up straight in the saddle and raising his Spencer in both hands. "You're a copper-riveted liar!"

Longarm had had enough. It was too cold and too early for this kind of bullshit, and he hadn't even had a cup of belly wash yet. He smoothly palmed his .44 and held it high, clicking back the hammer, and put the chill of the Dakota winter in his voice. "You fellas lower those goddamn rifles, and I ain't gonna tell ya twice."

He aimed his Colt at the old man, then wagged it back and forth between him and his sons. They'd all had their eyes riveted on Bone McCluskey, who was now wide-awake and still sitting against the cottonwood bole, held fast by the leg irons and the cuffs. The newcomers jerked their gazes to Longarm and sagged back in their saddles a little when they saw his hogleg bearing down on them.

"Damnit, his ass is ours, Marshal!" the husky younker spit out in frustration, his pale, fleshy cheeks showing some color even in the pale dawn light. "You should hear what ever'body's sayin' about Wanda. Hell, the preacher even rode his buggy out from town to tell us she can't come to church no more!"

"Ain't my fault!" McCluskey yelped. "Hell, the way she was waggin' that purty little ass around, any man woulda given her the shaft. No, sir, ain't my fault at all. A man can't be blamed for what a little vixen like that enticed him into." The scrawny outlaw chuckled bitterly. "Why, Wanda told me you boys even chased her around the barn a time or two. Her own *brothers*! With their *dicks* hangin' out! Only they weren't *hangin'*!"

"Why, you—!" The stocky younker gritted his teeth with fury as he raised his carbine to his shoulder.

Longarm aimed quickly. His .44 cracked loudly in the morning silence. His slug slammed into the forestock of the kid's carbine with an angry bark.

"Ach!" the kid yelped, throwing the gun away from him as though it had suddenly become hot. He entwined both gloved hands down low in front of him, cursing through clenched teeth.

Longarm aimed the cocked Colt at the old man, who sat glaring at him, nostrils expanding and contracting with blue fury.

Longarm filled his lungs. "As I said, I ain't gonna tell you fellas again. You turn around and ride on out of here, and I won't throw your mangy, perverted asses in the Bismarck hoosegow for interferin' with a federal lawman in the carryin' out of his duties."

He wasn't sure that was the correct charge language, as he'd never gotten accustomed to official blather, but it sounded good enough to him. It must have sounded good enough to the three men before him, too. The old man and the older boy dropped their beat-up carbines low across their pommels and gained wary, albeit indignant expressions on their hard, stupid faces.

"What're we gonna do, Pa?" the oldest boy asked tightly.

The old man continued to stare at the lawman for several stretched seconds, opening and closing his hands around his rifle. "I reckon we have to follow the law, boys." He took a deep breath. "Yessir, it's plain as the devil's Hell this badge toter ain't gonna turn that critter over to us . . . for proper disposal. Not much we can do about it, seein' as how he's a lawman an' all."

"But, Pa!" the oldest boy objected.

"Don't 'but, Pa' me, Edgar! What do ya want me to do—kill a federal lawman? Besides, he got us dead to rights, and he looks like he might be able to handle that hogleg o' his'n."

"Ah, shit!"

"Come on, boys," the old man said, keeping his owly gaze on Longarm as he reined his paint around. "We best get home, see to things back at the ranch."

With that, he spat chaw into the freshly fallen snow, turned forward, and put the steel to his horse. The paint galloped away from the creek, hooves thumping loudly on the frozen ground. The other two boys followed suit but they continued craning their necks to fix Longarm with hard, angry stares until the blue mist of dawn had nearly swallowed them.

Longarm depressed his Colt's hammer and dropped the piece into its holster. Snapping the keeper thong closed over the hammer, he turned and headed back through the trees to the fire. Bone's eyes were bright with fear as the outlaw sat with his hands cuffed between his thighs.

"Can you believe that?" The outlaw shook his head. "That little ole Wanda told them fellas I *savaged* her?"

Longarm tossed a log onto the glowing coals with a grunt. "Gettin' so you can't trust anyone anymore."

"And what galls me is that whole damn family is more inbred than a pack of mangy brush wolves!"

"I don't know," Longarm said, tossing another log on the fire, getting the blaze good and hot and ready to cook breakfast. "That oldest one looked like there might've been a randy Dutchman in the woodpile . . ."

He let his voice trail off. He'd heard something. Above the crackling and popping of the leaping flames, galloping hooves sounded in the north.

"Longarm, look out!" Bone shrieked.

The lawman wheeled to see a horse and rider galloping toward him through the trees. "Get him, boys!" the old man shouted, holding his Spencer repeater up tight against his shoulder as he drove the paint toward Longarm.

The rifle cracked, red orange flames stabbing.

The slug smacked a tree trunk behind the lawman. Bone bellowed.

The lawman crouched as he clawed the .44 from its holster and aimed quickly as the old man bore down on him, the paint's eyes flaring red in the firelight as it bulled through the brush toward Longarm.

Bone screamed, *"Look out, Longarm, goddamnit!"*

Longarm fired, then threw himself right. The horse's hammering left front hoof clipped his heel a half second before he hit the ground on his shoulder and rolled. He turned to see the paint leaping the fire with a shrill, bugling whinny as the old man flew left of his saddle, screaming, throwing both arms in the air and flinging the Spencer up amongst the branches.

"Pa!"

The cry rose amongst the clatter of two sets of hooves pounding toward Longarm. He looked up to see two horseback figures closing from either side, the horses twisting amongst the trees, the riders ducking under branches.

Guns popped. Bullets whizzed through the air, clipping twigs and plunking into tree boles.

Longarm gained a knee and fired two quick shots at the stocky lad hammering toward him while triggering an old Colt Navy in his gloved left fist. The kid was ten yards from Longarm when he gave a grunt and sagged back in his saddle, dropping both hands as though in supplication.

His horse stopped abruptly, front hooves skidding, sending the stocky younker tumbling over the mount's left hip. Longarm swung left to see the older boy approaching from thirty yards and closing fast, whooping at the top of his lungs like a rabid coyote caught in a springhouse.

He was triggering his rifle in one hand, a .44 Smith & Wesson in the other.

Longarm vaguely registered a sting, like that of a bee bite, in his low left side. He crouched and, gritting his teeth, emptied his .44 into the older boy's chest, then watched the still-howling firebrand roll ass over teakettle off his galloping mount's arched tail. The horse swung left, empty stirrups flapping like wings, eyes wide with fear and anger, and headed back north through the trees.

Its rider landed with a dull, crashing thud in a gooseberry thicket.

In the sudden silence in the wake of the gun clatter, Longarm heard the kid give a deep sigh and a low fart as he expired, belly down against the ground.

Longarm let his empty revolver sag against his side, and stared through the powder smoke wafting on the cold, gray air. He shuttled his gaze from the still figure of the oldest boy to that of his father piled up against a tree near the frozen creek. The old man lay jackknifed and twisted, his head at an angle that told Longarm the man's neck was broken. His head resting back against the base of the tree, he seemed to be smiling, weird blue eyes showing through the gradually brightening light.

The younger kid lay flat on his back over a deadfall cottonwood mantled with a thin snow layer. The kid's arms and legs jerked as his life dwindled.

"Crazy sons o' bitches," Longarm wheezed, automatically plucking the spent brass from his Colt Frontier and filling slugs the wheel with fresh slugs from his cartridge belt. He moved around stiffly, glancing around warily, half expecting more bushwhackers to bound toward him through the brush.

Too damn early for such nonsense. He hadn't been awake fifteen minutes, his brain still dream-fogged, and already three men lay dead around him.

For what?

Bone McCluskey?

Longarm heaved a disgusted sigh and moved over to the fire. On the other side, the outlaw sat against the cottonwood, head tipped back slightly, chin up, as though giving silent thanks to the good Lord for pulling him through another tight one.

"You know somethin', Bone?" Longarm said as he holstered his .44 and crouched over the low flames, reaching for a log beside the fire ring. "I'm beginning to wonder if you're worth the trouble of taking you back to Bismarck . . ."

The flames snapped. A distant magpie screeched.

Longarm dropped a log on the fire and glanced up, frowning at where the outlaw sat, oddly silent, against the cottonwood. The man was still staring up through the branches, cuffed hands resting in his lap, legs stretched straight out in front of him. His lower jaw hung slack, and his mouth was halfway open, lips covering his teeth.

Staring at the outlaw's still, silent form, Longarm tossed one more log on the fire, then went over and crouched before his prisoner. He waved a hand in front of the man's half-open eyes. Then he saw a thick blood drip on the side of Bone's neck, just below the earlobe.

Longarm canted his head for a better look. The blood trailed down from a hole just above the outlaw's left ear, partly concealed by hair and a large mole. Longarm reached up and grabbed a tuft of hair at the top of Bone's head, and pulled the man forward to look behind him.

The cottonwood bark was splattered with thick, dark red blood liberally speckled with brain and bone matter. The bullet must have ricocheted around inside the outlaw's head and exited the back. Longarm could see the slug embedded in the tree, at the dead center of all the gore.

"Well, shit." Longarm sighed as he pushed the dead man's head back against the tree. "Just like that I'm out a prisoner and the hangman in Bismarck is out a body to drop."

He started to push up off his haunches but stopped as a

wave of fatigue washed through him, pressing his shoulders down as though he'd suddenly been burdened by a heavy yoke. He felt a cold wetness low on his left side, and he clamped his hand to it, instantly feeling the blood staining his shirt.

Chapter 7

As he pressed his hand to the inky blood staining his side, Longarm remembered the bee sting he'd felt as the oldest boy had ridden toward him triggering a rifle and a six-shooter. The fireworks must have gotten him so heated up that he hadn't felt the wound at first.

But he felt it now, like a sharp, hot knife probing around between his ribs.

Quickly, he unbuttoned the lower power of his shirt and pulled the coarse wool away from his underwear top. Even more blood stained the red cotton of his long johns, pushing up slowly from the dime-sized hole about six inches up from his belt.

"Shit."

With a grunt, he pushed himself to his feet, then tramped over to the other side of the fire, sat down on his butt and sank back against his saddle. He reached into his saddlebags for his folding barlow knife and used the razor-edged blade to cut a large hole out of his underwear, exposing the small, ragged wound from which thick, dark red blood continued to ooze.

He reached around with his other hand to probe his lower back. No exit wound. The slug was still in there.

"You little privy snipe. I just hope sweet little ole Wanda appreciates what you did for her."

Longarm removed his red neckerchief, wadded it into a tight ball with a little tongue protruding, and, sucking a quick, deep breath and holding it, shoved the ball, tongue first, into the bullet hole. As the cloth was rammed into the tender wound, Longarm stretched his mustached lips back from his big, white teeth and called the three bushwhackers every epithet he could think of in both English and Spanish and finished off with a loud, shrill *"Son of a bitch!"*

Breathing hard and feeling sweat dribble down his cheeks, he sagged back against his saddle. When he'd caught his breath, he dug his bottle of cheap whiskey out of his saddlebags, popped the cork with his teeth, and threw back a pull that killed a good quarter of the bottle.

The whiskey hit his stomach and shot back up into his throat with a sizzling burn. But he gutted it out and sucked it down, and when he finally lowered the bottle to his thigh, he felt better for the effort.

A nice, dreamy gauze enveloped him, quelled the throbbing, icy burn in his side.

The cold of the morning tempered the whiskey, however, and he forced himself to consider his situation with some semblance of practicality. Returning the bottle to his saddlebags, he decided he needed to choke a bite of breakfast and coffee down, and then he needed to saddle his horse and light out in search of a sawbones or someone capable of digging the slug out.

He got the coffee cooking on a flat rock near the leaping flames and cast his gaze across the fire at Bone. A magpie was sitting on the outlaw's head, stomping around and lowering its black head to peruse the dead man's eyeballs as if trying to figure how it could reach the juicy, glazed orbs from his current position.

"Christ almighty," Longarm rasped, looking around for something to throw. "At least wait till he gets cold, will ya?"

He found a rock, whipped his fist back behind his shoulder, and slung the rock across the fire and chugging coffeepot. The magpie screeched and, awkwardly flapping its gaudy black, white, and translucent green wings, bolted straight up in the air.

At the same time, Longarm's rock struck Bone's forehead with a dull thud, then hit the ground and rolled. The outlaw's head jerked slightly, and his eyes appeared to blink.

Then his chin dropped slightly lower than before, eyes downcast, as though he were staring across his left shoulder now bloody from the leaking wound above his ear. Screeching angrily, the magpie flitted off through the high branches toward the gray sky that was lightening toward pearl.

Longarm grunted.

He dug the supper leftovers out of his saddlebags and took a few bites before pouring a cup of the piping hot belly wash. He drank down a third of the coffee, then filled the cup again with whiskey.

He sucked another half of the whiskey-laced coffee down, until a heightened sense of well-being and a further lessening of the pain in his side lightened his mood and steeled his resolve to ride. Then he heaved himself to his feet and walked off through the trees to his pinto tied beside McCluskey's paint.

Ten minutes later, he walked the saddled horse back up to the fire, McCluskey's paint, now free of its tether, plodding curiously along behind. Longarm tied his saddlebags onto the pinto's back behind his saddle, kicked dirt and rocks on the fire, then held the uncorked bottle up toward Bone in salute.

"Farewell, pardner. I'd try to get you in the ground, but, one, you don't deserve it, and, two, I reckon there's no point in us both saddlin' a cloud and ridin' double to the great hereafter."

With that he stepped into the pinto's saddle, holding his left forearm against his side, then triggered his Colt into the gauzy sky hovering just above the tops of the cottonwoods. Hauling back on the frightened pinto's reins, he glanced back at the paint.

He'd intended for the horse to hightail it away from here, in search of a new owner, which shouldn't be hard in ranch country. But aside from twitching its ears and curveting, the paint remained where it was, regarding Longarm skeptically from the side of its head.

"Have it your way."

Holstering the .44, he booted the pinto into the near-frozen creek. As he climbed the opposite bank, he glanced back to see the paint following about twenty yards behind—afraid, Longarm figured, to be left with a dead man. He didn't blame the mount a bit.

"Come on, hoss," he said as the pinto crested the bank, feeling better now that he had food and coffee in his belly. "More the merrier."

At the crest of the bank, he paused a moment to get his bearings and look around. There were few trails out here but horse trails, and most of those crisscrossed the country between ranches. Damn few towns, too. But heading back toward Bismarck the way he'd come, he should run into a little prairie burg in about thirty miles or so. He hadn't stopped in the town on his way north, so he didn't know what he'd find there, but he hoped like hell he'd find a medico or at least a dentist schooled in the fine art of lead fishing.

He booted the pinto forward and heard the paint blow and clomp along behind. He hadn't ridden fifty yards before the sun blossomed out of the eastern hogbacks like a giant yellow rose, instantly pressing its soothing heat against the back of Longarm's mackinaw and thawing his chilled blood. Steam tendrils rose from the light snow and the blond grass and wriggled across the ground like vaporous snakes.

A few puffy clouds rode low in the blue sky, but there was no sign of more snow anytime soon. He was glad about that. One good snow squall, in his weakened state, would do him in.

As he rode, trailed by the paint, he kept an eye skinned for a ranch or even a small farm where he might find someone able to dig the bullet out of his side. He saw a few cattle here and there, mostly mossy-horned mavericks holed up in draws, and plenty of old cow pies left by summer herds, but no ranchsteads.

Crossing a trail running southeast to northwest and marked with relatively recent wagon tracks, he considered following the trace, then nixed the idea. He might follow the trail in the wrong direction from the ranch headquarters, and he had little time to spare.

The farther he rode, stopping every couple of hours to water, grain, and rest his mount, the more he realized his time was running out. He was growing weaker, as though that yoke on his shoulders were growing heavier by the half hour, and he felt blood oozing out around the neckerchief and soaking his shirt, with icy rivulets inching down under his waistband and onto his hip and thigh.

He gave both himself and the horse a rest at midday. The paint stood nearby, munching wheatgrass from which the sun had melted nearly all the snow, and swishing its tail contentedly. Longarm considered shifting his saddle to the paint's back, to rest the pinto, but that idea he also had to nix. The maneuver would only cause the wound to bleed out more blood and make him weaker all the faster.

He wasn't sure how much blood a man had, but he could tell by the thick puddle on his shirt and over the pocket of his Levis that he'd probably lost a pint. Nibbling a second strip of jerky on a lone rock at the top of a low knoll, he put his face to the sun for a minute, then took a long look around.

He was surrounded by a rolling expanse of endless hogbacks, with here and there a flat-topped butte humping up in the misty distance. Frequent, shallow draws cut the prairie, and straight south there ran a line of barren trees sheathing a creek at the base of a jog of low, brown hills. Beyond that there wasn't much out here but the cool blue sky and warm sunlight angling between cottony clouds.

Hoping he remembered right about the town, he heaved himself from the rock with a groan and tightened the pinto's latigo cinch, then slipped the mount's bit back into its mouth. He turned a stirrup out, toed it, and pulled himself up into the hurricane deck, feeling as though he weighed an extra hundred pounds.

Boy, a bed was going to feel good.

Clucking to the horse, he set off once more, angling southwest, the paint plodding along lazily.

Longarm hadn't realized he'd dozed off until a whinny

woke him, and he lifted his head suddenly, looking around and blinking. The whinny had come from the trailing paint, and now the pinto whinnied, too.

Longarm's heart quickened, and he reached down to shuck his Winchester from his saddle boot. Usually he could cock the weapon one-handed, but now he had trouble levering a fresh shell into the breech even using both hands.

"What the fuck . . . ?"

Frowning, half expecting to spy Indians charging toward him, as the Sioux weren't all that happy with the white eyes of late, he swung his gaze from left to right and back again. He was on a high saddle between watersheds, and in the northeast he spied three winter-shaggy coyotes running up the side of a distant butte.

The lead coyote stopped suddenly and swung around toward Longarm. A big jack hung slack in his jaws. One of the other two moved up to clamp its own jaws around the rabbit, and the leader jerked his head away abruptly and continued up the hill.

In seconds, all three coyotes crested the butte and disappeared down the other side.

Longarm let the rifle sag in his arms as he depressed the hammer. "Christ," he growled, shuttling a wry glance between the paint and the pinto. "What a couple of Nancy boys you two are . . . frightened by a couple of brush wolves a half mile away and headin' home with supper."

Sliding the Winchester back into its boot, he nudged the pinto with his heels. The horse twitched its ears, shook its head, and set out once more. The paint gave one more, halfhearted whinny, as though in protest of Longarm's estimation of his character.

Up and down the prairie hogbacks they rode, the two

horses and the pinto's intermittently dozing rider. Suddenly, Longarm was awakened by his own snoring, and he lifted his head abruptly. He blinked as he stared down at the pinto who, inexplicably, had his head over a stock trough and was loudly drawing water. The paint stood to Longarm's right, at a hitch rail flanking the stock tank. The paint, too, was drawing the black, hay-and ice-flecked water into its snout.

Longarm looked around, his neck so stiff that he could hear the bones creak. A deep frown mantled his steel-blue eyes, and the ends of his longhorn mustache rose above both mouth corners. While he'd been fast asleep in the saddle, the pinto had carried him to the far eastern edge of a little town.

Chapter 8

Before Longarm sat a small, wood-frame building, not much more than a square box with a peaked roof and with a faded sign over the front door announcing JACK JOHNSON, SADDLE MAKER & GUNSMITH. A couple of yellowed wanted posters were tacked between the large window and the door, which was crowned with bleached deer antlers. It was the first building on the north side of the town's broad, dusty main drag.

To his left, lining both sides of the street, were about a dozen or so buildings similar to the harness shop—some bigger, some smaller, a couple constructed of adobe bricks and some boasting tent canvas on their second stories. There were large gaps between most of the buildings, as though the founding fathers were afraid they wouldn't have enough structures to fill out their town and hold the wind at bay, so they spaced them widely. Most of the gaps boasted woodpiles or trash heaps, and paper and wood chips danced in the cool breeze funneling down the street from the west.

Reeling a little in the saddle, light-headed, Longarm returned his gaze to the harness shop. He wanted to inquire about a sawbones, but the big, flyspecked window was dark, and a shade was pulled down over the small window in the door. There was no one else on the street—just one lone dog trotting toward Longarm from the far side of town. The medium-sized yellow mutt walked sort of crooked, tail and tongue hanging.

As it stopped abruptly and backed up to sniff a smell it had nearly passed over, Longarm turned the pinto away from the water trough and regarded the livery barn on the opposite side of the street. HARVEY LIVERY AND STOCK BARN read the large, faded green letters sprawled across the second story. The broad doors were closed, as was the smaller door to their right side.

What the hell? Longarm thought. Had he lost track of the days and landed here on a Sunday? No, he was sure it was Friday.

Where the hell was everybody? He'd only seen towns this forlorn in the paths of raging wildfires. Smoke wafted from most of the tin chimney pipes and brick smokestacks. Somebody was here. He raked his gaze left and right and back again, but he spied saw no sign for a medico.

There was a broad, yellow, two-story building at the center of town on the south side of the street, with a sign over its roofed porch that announced HOCKENSMITH HOTEL & MERCANTILE. Small cursive letters angling down off the end of "mercantile" announced, as if with chagrin, SPIRITS AND BEER. Smoke billowed from several chimneys bristling from the place's multilevel roof.

Definitely folks over there.

Longarm clucked to the pinto and angled toward the big building spewing the most smoke in town. The dog, who had continued toward Longarm again, stopped suddenly to show its teeth and raise its hackles. Longarm heard the low growls on the chill breeze. As the pinto approached the tie rack fronting the hotel–mercantile, the dog wheeled suddenly and headed back the way it had come, tail down, glancing cautiously back over its shoulder at the strange, slouching rider.

Longarm half fell out of his saddle. He unbuckled the pinto's belly cinch, slipped its bit from its mouth. Clutching his wounded side, where the blood was cold and clammy against his skin and he felt as though he'd been stuck with a rusty pigsticker, he climbed the porch's seven steps and thumped to the glassed front door.

He pushed the door open, hearing the cowbell over his head clatter raucously, and stopped abruptly, one foot over the threshold, as he watched a good half dozen male faces jerk toward him suddenly. Expressions ranging from surprise to disdain shone in the bearded faces beneath scruffy Stetsons.

A couple of hands drifted to sidearms, of which there were plenty. In fact, every rough-garbed man in the room appeared to have at least one pistol in addition to the Spencers or Winchesters resting across tables or empty chairs.

No one said anything as they sat around tables scattered along the left side of the room and around a big, potbelly stove that ticked and chugged with a sizable fire. The right side of the room was devoted to dry-goods shelves, bins, and barrels. Straight back in the misty shadows at the end of the long, dark room that smelled like pine smoke, molasses, sausage, and new cotton, a slender, aproned gent with a thick black mustache and black pomaded hair stood behind planks propped on flour barrels.

He stood so statue-still that for a moment Longarm wondered if the man were alive. Maybe he'd been shot by these cow waddies or drifters or desperadoes or whoever the hell they were and propped there to spook newcomers.

Longarm continued inside and closed the door behind him. His face was expressionless as he moved straight back through the tables, holding his head forward but aware of all eyes following him as playing cards were held in still hands and tobacco smoke curled toward the wainscoted ceiling.

In the heavy silence, his boots thumped loudly on the broad, scratched puncheons of the squeaky floor. As he approached the bar, he saw a man sitting at a table with three others cast a hard, admonishing stare toward the tables near the front of the room. A couple of chairs scraped back, and in a cracked mirror behind the bar, Longarm watched two men in blanket coats hurry through the door and outside, the bell jingling raucously once more.

Longarm hoped he'd just walked into a passel of ranch hands in town for a friendly game of cards, nothing more. But all signs so far led to something far more sinister.

Damn, he hated the north country. When hadn't he had bad luck up here?

"Help you, mister?" the barkeep asked tensely, quietly, resting his long, pale hands lightly atop the bar planks.

"Whiskey." Longarm flipped a quarter onto the bar and leaned forward. He was so light-headed he was worried he might pass out in the midst of these curly wolves, who might very well commence feeding on his beat-up old carcass.

The barman turned stiffly to grab a bottle and a shot glass from the shelves behind him. Glancing over Longarm's shoulder at the curly wolves, he set the glass on the bar planks, plucked the cork from the bottle, and poured whiskey with more care than necessary into the glass.

His face was taut and expressionless, his skin pasty. He appeared ailing, but Longarm could almost smell the man's anxiousness.

Longarm glanced into the mirror behind the apron again.

The other patrons were shifting around in their chairs and casting incredulous glances at each other, most eyes drawn to the man who'd thrown the hard, commanding look that had sent the two men outside—a burly gent with a head bald as an egg, a red goatee that stuck out six inches from his chin, and bushy red sideburns. He was fair-skinned and lightly freckled, with little blue pig eyes that glowed in the light from the window beside him.

He wore fringed deerskin breeches, a red bandanna, and a pin-striped shirt, with a wool-lined mackinaw draped over his chair back. Two big, silver-chased pistols rode high on his hips, one positioned for the cross draw.

A Winchester repeater leaned against his table, which he shared with two other rough-looking hombres, all three holding cards in their hands. The three had resumed their game but with a brooding, distracted air.

Longarm grunted softly as a pain spasm racked him, and he threw back the whiskey. The liquor braced him like a slap from a snowmelt stream. He shivered and his knees went soft, and when he got himself under control again, feeling strong but knowing it wouldn't last, he rested one elbow on the bar and regarded the nervous apron with a casual air.

"This town got a sawbones?"

The barman's bushy, salt-and-pepper brows furrowed slightly. He spoke tightly, softly. "It does."

"I'd like a room." Longarm tossed a silver cartwheel

onto the bar planks. "Then I'd like you to send someone for the sawbones. Send 'em to my room."

Leaning on his elbow, the lawman poured himself a fresh drink. The barman stood as still as before, as though his shoes were cemented to the puncheons. Longarm glanced up at the man from beneath his chestnut brows.

"You understand English, friend?"

The apron swallowed and shifted his gaze between the bald man behind Longarm and the lawman himself, obviously conflicted.

"Uh . . ." someone said behind him, drawing it out slowly for menacing emphasis, ". . . the hotel here is done filled up. Too bad it's the only hotel in Harvey. Oh, well." In the mirror behind the apron, the bald man yawned and tossed a card onto his table, not looking at Longarm as he added, "You'll have to keep ridin', stranger. Best of luck to ye. Hope you're feeling' better reeel soon."

As the man beside the bald man tossed a card down, the bald man casually plucked a quirley from an ashtray and took a long, leisurely drag.

"Some o' you boys'll have to double up," Longarm said, staring at the miserable apron. "I'll take that key now, mister."

Behind Longarm, two chairs scraped across the puncheons, the noise booming in the quiet, cavernous room that was made more quiet by the clouds that had moved in outside, and the light snow that had begun to fall beyond the windows.

"I'll also need someone to tend my horses," Longarm said, still staring at the apron but noting the two men rising from chairs near the front of the room and slowly swaggering toward him, bat-wing chaps flapping about their legs. “Pinto and a paint. Can’t miss ’em. Have ’em grained and rubbed down good.”

The apron glanced behind Longarm and made a face as though he’d just swallowed a lemon wedge. “Look, mister, maybe you’d better . . .”

He let his voice trail off as he glanced over Longarm’s shoulder, at the two men approaching the bar side by side and peeling their coat flaps back from the pistols on their hips. Longarm did not turn around, but continued to lean on one elbow, his left hand wrapped around his filled shot glass.

In the mirror behind the frozen apron, he watched the two men come up behind him and stop and bore holes into his back with their hard, cow-dumb eyes. They were both long-haired and bearded. One wore a bowler hat and a scar across his forehead while the other wore a black felt hat with a floppy brim and a bullet crown.

Except for the creaking woodstove, the place had fallen as silent as a snow-shrouded tomb.

One of the men behind Longarm raised his arm. Longarm felt the man’s finger poke his left shoulder blade. The man cleared his throat.

Longarm lifted his shot glass and tossed back the shot. It hadn’t finished searing his tonsils when, flipping the glass so that it fit snug in his palm, the hard round bottom of the glass protruding slightly from the bottom of his fist, he wheeled quickly, swinging his filled left fist around behind him.

In spite of the hole in his side, Longarm had moved so quickly that the man who’d tapped the lawman’s shoulder hadn’t had time to wipe the smug, condescending look off his face before Longarm did it himself as the shot glass and Longarm's fist slammed into the man's left temple with a solid smack of stout glass against hard bone.

"Achh!" the man cried, staggering back and raising his hands to his head as the glass bounced off his shoulder, then hit the floor with a ringing thud.

Before the other man had time to react, Longarm whipped around in the opposite direction, grabbing the whiskey bottle from the bar planks thumb down and slamming the bottle against the second gent's right temple. The bottle must have been made of lesser stuff than the glass. It shattered and sprayed whiskey in all directions as the second man screamed wildly and stumbled to Longarm's right, his knees buckling, his bowler hat tumbling onto the floor where he kicked it.

"Son of a bitch!" the first man cried as, setting his feet under him and clamping one hand to his bloody temple, he clawed iron.

Longarm's .44-40 was already up, cocked, and aimed. It leaped and barked, rocking the entire room, making glass sing and dust sift from the rafters.

"Yoww!" the first man said as Longarm's bullet hammered into the man's soft leather holster, ricocheting off the man' hogleg to bury itself in one of the barrels holding up the bar to Longarm's left. The man squeezed his gun hand with his other hand, raising it to chest level and regarding Longarm with red-eyed fury. "Son of a *bitch*!"

Thinking twice about reaching for the second pistol sticking up from a silver-trimmed holster over his belly, he shifted his exasperated gaze from Longarm's face to his cocked .44, then back to the lawman's eyes again.

Longarm caught a glimpse of movement behind the man facing him. His Colt leaped and roared once more.

The man who'd been raising a long-barreled Remington from the far side of the table at which the group's leader was sitting loosed a screech and grabbed his upper right arm. Dropping the Remy, he jerked back in his chair, cursing through a white-toothed grimace that lifted his bushy, brown mustache and reddened his broad, pitted cheeks.

Once more, Longarm's pistol roared.

The quirley that had been resting in the ashtray of the group's leader disappeared as the ashtray bounced off the table and leaped back over the bald's man's left shoulder. It slammed against the wall and hit the floor with a dull thud.

The bald man, who'd dropped both hands beneath the table, shoulders rolling slightly as he went for one of his own silver-chased six-shooters, froze. He stared at Longarm grimly from beneath his shaggy red brows.

"Mister, you got cojones, I'll give you that." The bald man's voice was deep and teeming with barely restrained fury. "But there ain't no way you can get us all."

Several other men jerked up from their chairs.

Chapter 9

Ka-boooom!

In the close confines, the shotgun blast sounded like two planets colliding.

Longarm had just started to aim his Colt at one of the other men clawing iron on the tail of their bald-headed leader's menacing, accurate statement. But as the floor shifted around beneath his boots and the concussion hit his ears like the slap of cupped hands, he held his fire.

More dust sifted from the rafters. Outside, a dog barked.

A woman's voice yelled, *"Enough!"*

The other men in the room—all twelve—froze in crouches over their chairs, their hands curled around the grips of their six-shooters or rifle stocks. Longarm frowned over the barrel of his cocked, extended .44, thin white smoke curling from the maw.

A girl whom he'd missed when he'd entered the mercantile–hotel–saloon stood behind a table ahead and to Longarm's left, in front of a couple of candy barrels and coarse, pale wheels of goat cheese hanging from a ceiling beam. She was a thin little thing with long curly brown hair falling to her shoulders, and with a brown-eyed, oval face featuring a straight nose and bee-stung, red lips. Like Cinnamon, she was pretty in a tomboyish way, though she wore a simple gray dress under a heavy wool poncho, with white camisole hems showing below the dress.

Apparently she wore her twelve-gauge barn blaster from a sling beneath the poncho, for the wool garment was pulled up now above the gut shredder's smoking left barrel.

"No killin'!" the girl said, her voice at once husky and feminine as she raked her angry gaze back and forth across the room. "I done told ya," she added, before shuttling her gaze toward the bald-headed man still frozen in the same position as before, both hands beneath his table, his blue pugnacious eyes on Longarm. "Jethro, what'd I tell you?"

The bald man's face flushed above his goatee and between his shaggy sideburns. "Alma, goddamnit, it was this here tall drink o' pisswater that clawed iron."

The girl turned her head toward Longarm. "Only after you sicced Boony and Vern on him. Everybody put away your damn guns and relax. Like I done told y'all, there'll be no unnecessary killin'. Just the job, and that's all."

Her dark brown eyes dropped to Longarm's bloody coat and thigh, then rose again to his face. She wagged the shotgun up and down, beetling her thin brown eyebrows and keeping her voice hard and commanding. "That goes for you, too, mister . . . unless you wanna end up part of the wall behind ya."

Longarm glanced behind her and around her. Jethro and the other hard cases looked cowed as mongrels caught burying bones in a garden patch. They'd all sagged back down in their chairs, horns pulled in, hands away from their guns.

Longarm flipped his .44 into its holster but left the keeper thong free. The girl stood about two feet in front of him, canting her pretty, delicate, brown-eyed head slightly to give him a brash up and down. "You heard the man, Mr. Halstead," she purred. "Give him a room."

"Alma!" objected Jethro, bunching his whiskered lips and forehead so that he resembled nothing so much as an enraged bulldog teased by an unflappable cat.

The girl smiled up at Longarm. "And you'd better send your boy for that sawbones."

"Alma!"

"Hurry, Mr. Halstead. We wouldn't want the tall stranger to bleed himself dry on the floor!"

Halstead nervously plucked a key from a rack behind him, then extended it toward Longarm, the apron's hand shaking as though with the ague.

Longarm turned to take the key, but the girl stepped up beside him. "I'll take that."

"Alma, goddamnit!"

"Oh, hush, Jethro," she said, still smiling beguilingly up at the lawman towering over her. She plucked the key from the barman's palm. "You can be such a bore sometimes."

Holding her shotgun under her arm, Alma moved past Longarm and stepped around the end of the bar, swiveling her head to regard him over her shoulder. "Follow me, stranger. Don't worry—I've got your back."

Longarm glanced at Jethro and the other hard cases, then, keeping his eyes on the room and his hand on his pistol's grips, he sidled around the bar and followed the girl to a narrow, freestanding stairs rising steeply into dense shadows. "Room twelve," the girl said as she climbed the stairs ahead of Longarm, holding her skirts above her ankle-high black boots, her bottom appearing small and round and alluring under all that wool. "That's right next to mine—the only one not occupied."

Longarm felt as though his boots were filled with mud, but he managed to gain the second story without fainting. The girl glanced over her shoulder again to make sure he was still behind her.

"Going to make it?" she asked, turning her head forward as she strolled down the dark, narrow hall, the walls paneled in bare lumber with here and there a mounted candle lamp. Most of the candles were burnt down to nubs.

Longarm clomped along behind her, his left hand clamped over the wound that had stopped bleeding for a time but now, likely because of the high jinks downstairs, had opened up again.

The girl frowned up at him as she turned the key in a lock. "Don't say much, do ya?"

"What's to say?"

The lock clicked. She turned the knob and threw open the door with an ironic flourish. "Got me there."

Longarm stepped inside. There was a bed, a small dresser, a marble-topped washstand, a beat-up chest of drawers, and a charcoal brazier in one corner. A green lamp sat on the dresser. The whipsawed pine boards lining the room were unadorned except for two bullet holes placed about six inches apart, and what looked like dry blood staining the wood around them.

Longarm walked over to the bed and sat down gingerly. He swiped his hat from his head and eased himself back against the brass headboard. He grunted and grimaced as more blood oozed from the hole in his shirt, and threw the flaps of his coat back to better inspect the wound.

There wasn't much to see through his shirt, however, except blood.

Leaving the door open, the girl strolled over to the bed and frowned down at the lawman's bloody shirt. "You're a mess, stranger. Best get outta them duds. The doc might be a while. Heard he's one o' them bottle doctors."

Longarm leaned forward and dropped a shoulder to remove his coat. "Nice to know."

After Longarm had struggled for a time with the heavy mackinaw, realizing he should have taken the coat off before he'd collapsed on the bed, Alma said, "Here, here."

She leaned her shotgun against the wall and peeled the coat back off his shoulders. Longarm sat up, groaning sharply as another bowie knife of searing pain cleaved his middle, and the girl yanked the coat off his arms.

Suddenly, he remembered that he'd stuffed his badge into his coat pocket. He glanced at the coat, inwardly wincing as she tossed it onto a chair. The badge didn't clatter against the chair or fall out of the pocket. Relief swept him. If the gang found out he was a lawman—and if they were the outlaws he figured them to be—he wouldn't have a whore's chance in hell of surviving sundown.

Alma shoved him back against the headboard. "Now, the shirt . . ."

The girl sat on the bed beside him, curling one leg under her thigh while keeping her other foot on the floor. Leaning toward him, she began unbuttoning his shirt. She looked into his eyes from a foot away, her own eyes at once vaguely flirtatious and challenging.

A real piece of work. Longarm bet she'd carved a broad swath of broken hearts in her young life—probably not yet twenty.

Longarm gave her a hard, appraising look, and then he reached up and grabbed one of her wrists. She frowned.

"Who's Jethro?" he asked.

She raised a brow. "I thought we had nothing to say. Personally, I've always considered short conversations best with men."

"You have, have you?"

"You don't strike me as much of a talker, mister, umh . . . ?"

Longarm gave a snort and released her wrist. He wasn't going to get anything out of her. He was in no condition to do anything about the gang anyway, whatever gang they were and whatever they were up to here in Harvey, Dakota Territory. Judging by the deserted streets and by the demeanor of the bartender downstairs, they had the town thoroughly cowed.

Maybe they'd robbed a bank or were waiting for a stage to rob.

Alma continued unbuttoning his shirt until she was down to his cartridge belt. Leaning even closer to him and biting her lower lip, she pulled his shirttails out of his trousers, grunting softly, her eyes smoky. Then she unbuttoned the last two buttons and swept the bloody shirt back from his bloody longhandle top, exposing the wound from which the blood-soaked handkerchief protruded.

The girl shook her head and sucked in her cheeks. "Don't look good, stranger. Who shot you, anyway?"

"Some farm hag caught me stealin' potatoes from her garden patch."

"The bullet still in there?"

"Think so. Do me a favor and pour me a glass of water, will ya? Then you can vamoose. I know you got better things to do downstairs than tend the sick and wicked. The sawbones should be staggerin' in just any old time."

Alma got up and walked over to the washstand upon which a pitcher, water glass, and washbasin sat. "What makes you think I got better things to do downstairs?"

"Just the climate of the place."

"What climate is that?"

Longarm hiked a shoulder as the girl splashed water into the glass. "Edgy. Sorta like a cow camp with Injuns on the prod."

"Aren't you observant."

"Been called worse."

"I bet you have." Alma brought the glass of water over and, while Longarm drank, she returned to the washstand. She splashed water from the pitcher into the basin, grabbed a towel from a peg at the side of the stand, and returned to the bed, where she sank down next to Longarm. Lowering her head and nibbling her lip, she began working on the buttons of his longhandle top.

Longarm snorted. "Kind of forward, ain't ya?"

"Some say so."

When she'd worked her way down to the lawman's cartridge belt, she peeled the bloody top off his shoulders, laying his chest bare. Her eyes scuttled across his broad shoulders and the twin, hard slabs of his pectorals lightly carpeted in chestnut hair, and the color rose in her cheeks. "I must say, you're a fine chunk of maleness, stranger." She glanced at the wound from which the bloody, balled neckerchief protruded. "Should take better care of yourself."

Longarm opened his mouth to respond but merely sucked a sharp breath as the girl abruptly plucked the handkerchief, crusted with dried blood, from the wound. She might as well have thrown burning kerosene on him.

"Jesus H. Christ!" Longarm grimaced, rolling his head around on his shoulders. "What the hell'd you do that for?"

"Had to come out sooner or later." She set the bloody rag in the basin, then dampened a corner of the towel.

As she moved the damp towel toward the wound, Longarm grabbed her hand. "I think I'll take my chances with the medico, if that's all right with you."

"Oh, hush," the girl said, jerking her hand free. "If you had any idea how many wounds I've tended, you wouldn't even see no need for the medico. Hell, I could dig that slug out of you as good as he could and"—her sultry brown eyes flicked up toward his—"you might have a whole lot better time in the process."

Just then, boots thudded on the stairs beyond the closed door.

The girl pulled the towel away from Longarm's side and turned the corners of her mouth down. "Well, there's your medico. Better hope he's sober."

She set the towel and the basin on the bed and gained her feet as three quick knocks on the door sounded. She pulled open the door, then wheeled with a flourish, throwing an arm out to indicate the lawman, her long, curly hair bouncing about her shoulders.

"There's your patient, Doc. If you need any help, just yell." She blew Longarm a kiss, winked, then strode out the open door as a short, stocky gent in a black suit and bowler hat walked in, a leather kit in his hand, a stogie wedged between his teeth.

The man stopped just inside the door, blinking dully. His suety, clean-shaven face was expressionless, but his deep, gravelly voice teemed with sarcasm. "Hope I wasn't interruptin' anything. I can come back later. It's just that Halstead's boy pulled me away from a card game back of the café where I was fifty dollars ahead—and I ain't seen fifty dollars all at one time in nearly as many years—so I figured it was important."

Longarm pressed the towel to the bullet hole. "Matter of fact, you might've already saved my life, Doc. Come on over. Don't be shy. Took a bullet right here, and I reckon I'd be dead if my liver was on the wrong side."

The doctor set his kit on the bed, then doffed his hat, removed his coat, and loosened his tie. Giving the tie another tug, he regarded Longarm suspiciously, and canted his head at the door. "You one o' them?"

"Nope."

The man frowned down at him, bushy gray brows beetled curiously. "Newcomer?"

"Just rode in. Had me a nice, warm welcome downstairs, then the girl, Alma, took me up here and all but clawed the bullet out with her fingers."

"That's a wildcat, that one," the medico said, rolling up his sleeves. "Didn't catch your name."

"George Long." Longarm didn't know who he could trust around here, so he'd decided to go by a phony name until he got a handle on the situation, and he found himself in a condition to take action or defend himself again, whichever need arose first.

"I'm Doc Cranston. Ezekial Cranston, at your service." The doctor set a pair of steel-rimmed spectacles on his nose and removed the towel from over Longarm's bullet hole. "Didn't figure on anyone gettin' into town, the way they been watchin' the main road."

"Who are they?"

"Mantooth Bunch. Jethro and his wicked little sis, Alma, run an outlaw ranch down around the Sagebrush River."

"She's that bulldog's sister?" Longarm emphasized sister, sucking a sharp breath, as the doctor, leaning forward over the lawman's belly, prodded the bullet hole with his fingers.

"Half sister. Jethro's pa killed Alma's ma, but somehow they stayed close . . . close as two wild coyotes, I reckon, and took to rustlin' and stagecoach robbin' along with runnin' about a hundred head of beef on their coyote ranch amongst the river buttes. Been runnin' wild around here for years, shootin' up the town once or twice a year. When we see 'em comin' we call the place Helldorado. 'Well, looks like it's gonna be Helldorado around here tonight, fellas. Best keep your women and children to home.' "

Cranston glanced up and over his small, round spectacles at Longarm's face. "How long ago did this happen, anyways? I don't like your color."

"This mornin'. I rode in an hour ago."

"My guess is you were forted up in a line shack with some hombre, and you had a conflict over cards or a woman or both, or maybe one of you just got stir-crazy and drunk and started shootin'." Cranston opened his kit and pulled out a half-full whiskey bottle. "I see it all the time out here."

"Close enough, Doc."

Longarm reached for the bottle as Cranston popped the cork. The doctor frowned and jerked the bottle out of the lawman's reach, then threw back several long, gurgling shots himself. The old man's Adam's apple bobbed like a cork in a mountain stream, with a hooked fish jerking from below.

"Shit," Longarm said through a grimace. "The girl wasn't whistlin' Dixie about you bein' a bottle doctor."

Cranston pulled the bottle down, running his forearm across his mouth. "How dare she call me that! I delivered that little polecat!"

He handed the bottle to Longarm, who, regarding the sawbones skeptically as the man rummaged around in his medical kit, threw back a couple of liberal shots of the who-hit-John. He had to swallow hard to keep the snakewater from coming back up again. He thought he could taste the gunpowder and snake heads from which it was no doubt concocted, but it did the trick, soothing though far from obliterating the throbbing, fiery pain in his side.

When he saw the wicked-looking instruments the medico produced from his war bag—a protractor and a forceps, both somewhat rusty—he took another long, desperate pull from the bottle. If he made it out of this country alive—and his chances were looking slimmer all the time—he'd never again accept an assignment north of Cheyenne.

Mostly to keep his mind off the forthcoming horror, Longarm said, "Ain't there no law around here?"

Cranston shook his head as he held the instruments over the washbasin and doused them with whiskey. "None to speak of. There's a sheriff over to Rugby, but it's a big county, and he hardly ever makes it over this way."

Longarm rested his head back against his pillow propped up against the brass headboard and stared at the smoke-stained ceiling. "Seems to me they're waitin' around for somethin'. Or someone."

"Me and the other townsmen feel the same way. Mantooth and his boys and Alma been here three days now, millin' around between the saloon here and the whorehouse up the street a ways. Jethro and Alma done posted sentries at both ends of the main drag, and they ain't lettin' anyone in or out . . .'cept for you. They musta let their guard down for a time."

Cranston glanced at Longarm sharply, holding up the rusty protractor for emphasis. "Now, you know there's gotta be some reason for that, but I tell you, I don't even *wanna* know what it is. And, Mr. Long, you best hightail it fast as you can once I dig that bullet out of your hide."

Longarm snorted dryly, keeping up the hard-luck drifter charade. "Don't have to tell me twice!"

"Better take another pull from the bottle before I start scrounging around for the slug."

Longarm groaned, threw back another long pull, then corked the bottle and propped it beside him.

"Oh, wait." Cranston dipped a hand into his bag again, producing a thick scrap of well-chewed rawhide. "Best bite down on that so you don't crack your teeth. There ain't a dentist within sixty miles of here."

Longarm clamped the rawhide between his teeth, then reached up to grab the headboard's brass spools. "Let's get it over with," he said around the rawhide.

Cranston hunkered down over Longarm's belly, and when the lawman felt the tools sliding inside the wound, he bit down on the hide and lifted his gaze to the ceiling. He was prepared for the worst; he'd had lead dug out of him before, and having it plucked from his torso had proven the most painful of all extractions.

So he was surprised when, after only a few seconds of fishing around with the protractor and forceps, the doctor dropped both instruments into the basin, jabbed his thumb and index finger into the wound for only a second before raising his hand with a bloody slug pinched between bloody fingers.

"Damn," the doctor croaked. "It was only in there a couple of inches, real close to the hole. Must've bounced off a coupla ribs. A thirty-caliber, looks like. Huh." He dropped the slug in the basin, then washed his hands in the bloody water. "What do you know? I could've tore you up real bad if it was in there very far."

Longarm lowered his hands from the headboard and spit out the rawhide. "That's it?"

"Exept for cleanin' you out and sewin' you up." With a hand stained with bloody water, the doctor picked up the bottle once more, threw another shot down his throat, then rammed the lip of the bottle into the wound.

Longarm lifted his head, eyes nearly popping out of his head, as the whiskey plunged into him, feeling like the poisoned tip of a Kiowa war lance cleaving him straight through.

"Ohh-ahhhh! Jezuzzzz Chriiiiiist!"

Chapter 10

Longarm was wonderfully, graciously pie-eyed by the time the sawbones, who'd sent down for another bottle to split between him and his patient, had finished cleaning out and sewing up the wound. The man staggered out of the room with his medical kit, and before he'd latched the door behind him, Longarm was asleep.

He awoke in a semi-stupor when someone entered his room, now dark with snow ticking against the window-panes, to drop his tack and rifle on the floor beside the dresser. He was vaguely aware of a young boy's voice muttering, "And I'll take that tip in the mornin', you lousy snipe . . ."

Then the door clicked shut, boots scuffed off down the hall, and Longarm's eyelids closed once again.

He stirred slightly after that, to the pounding and scraping of drunken feet in the hall outside his room, to bodies thumping against the wall, and raucous drunken bellows. Even in his sleep, anxiety bit down on him hard. In his condition, he was defenseless against the Mantooth Bunch, should they decide to get shed of the stranger, or if one of them recognized him. He'd been a lawman long enough to have acquired an extensive reputation, and he'd rubbed shoulders with a lot of hombres, most of them bad.

When his door opened suddenly, and he heard a girl cry—"Same to you, ya fuckin' limp-dicked weasel! I wouldn't spread my legs for your mangy noodle if it was the last dick in the territory!"—he groaned and flung a hand toward the right bedpost, where he normally would have hung his gun and cartridge belt. He clawed only air, however. In his agonized, drunken state, he'd dropped his gun rig somewhere on the dark floor below the bed, well out of his reach in his current condition, unless he wanted to open up the stitches and bleed his life out on the sheets.

The door slammed so loudly that the bed jumped and the walls shuddered. The hall's dim candlelight bled through the cracks around the frame and through the keyhole, silhouetting a slender figure in front of it.

"Who's there?" Longarm drawled. All the hooch he'd tossed down his gullet, on an empty stomach and low on blood, made the room pitch and sway around him, and small flares burst in his eyes.

Alma giggled. There were several scrapes and clomps as she staggered around the room, and then a solid thump, like a boot hitting the floor. That was followed by a hollow bang and a thump, as though a boot had bounced off the wall before hitting the puncheons. A spur rang softly.

"Go 'way," Longarm choked. "This is a private goddamn room. I paid fer it . . . and I demand my piracy."

The girl laughed huskily amidst the sibilant sounds of jostling clothes. "Piracy?"

She laughed again.

Longarm was propped on his elbows, feeling as defenseless as a toddler in a bassinet amongst a raiding party of drunken Kiowa.

"Ran into the doc," the girl said, breathless, still staggering around and shedding clothes. Now that his eyes had adjusted, he could see her more clearly and smell the smoke and hooch wafting around her. "You ain't in bad shape, he says. Of course, he was three sheets to the wind . . ."

"Yeah, well, ain't we all. Now, l-leave me alone, girl. I ain't in the mood for whatever you got in mind. Come back in the horning, and we'll talk about it then."

"Hornin' in the morrow." The girl laughed. "I like that! But you know what, stranger? Turns out Alvin and Joe Wiley got all mad at each other during their poker game earlier, and they refuse to sleep in the same room together."

She gave a grunt as she jerked a garment over her head. "So Alvin took my room, and I refuse to sleep with that fat pervert. I'd go in an' sleep with my brother, but I can't say as I trust him, neither, even after the two whores he just diddled over at the Purple Pleasure Palace. Besides, he snores like a grizzly dreamin' of springtime pussy!

"Whoops!"

Longarm saw her jerk and weave, apparently slipping on her own clothes strewn about the floor. Then, chuckling, she padded around the end of the bed and came up from the other side, whipping the covers back. Her body was a cream oval in the darkness, and he could hear her teeth clattering.

"Cold tonight, stranger." The bed squawked as she climbed onto it, breathing hard and pulling the sheets and quilts up. "And I need me a tall, dark stranger to keep me warm."

Another objection died stillborn on Longarm's lips as the girl rolled toward him and snaked her arms around his neck. Her cool, lithe body was smooth as silk, her lips soft and moist as she kissed his cheek and nuzzled his neck before nibbling his earlobe.

He was so cocooned in drunken gauze that he couldn't tell for sure, but he thought he detected a pinprick of pleasure in his loins, like a charge of low-level electricity. What he did know for sure was the girl's body was warming up quickly as she wrapped her legs around his and clung to him tightly, shivering, her long, swirling hair caressing his shoulder, and that he was starting not to mind it.

As long as she didn't expect any horseplay, which he had not the strength for.

"All right, now," he grunted. "I gotta sleep. Your old bottle doctor just fished a slug outta my hide. Need some healin' time."

"Don't mind me," Alma said, her voice a hot growl against his neck. "I'm just here to get some shut-eye and sleep off the pond of coffin varnish I drank while I fleeced my brother and a coupla the other boys at stud." Longarm clenched as her cool hand found his cock that, he realized as her fingers closed around it, was as hard as the iron driveshaft on a Baldwin locomotive.

The girl was as surprised as he was. "Hey, what the hell is *this*?" She squeezed him again, running her hand up and down his hard length, from the bulging mushroom to the base. "I thought you were *injured*!"

"Don't let it fool you," Longarm growled. "I'm in a bad . . . way . . ."

He let the sentence drift off as she ran her hand up from his balls to the tip of his cock once more. "Christ almighty, what kinda club you got under there, stranger?"

She pulled her head away from his neck and stared into his eyes, her brown orbs sparkling eagerly in the darkness. "Mind if I take a peek? I just wanna *look*. I won't do nothin' if you don't *want* me to."

Before Longarm could respond, she'd ducked down under the covers, tenting the blankets over his waist. She said something that he couldn't make out under there, and then he felt—what was it, her nose?—running down his fully engorged length before her flicking tongue caressed his balls.

"Oops, sorry," she said, peeking out from under the blankets with an expression of false chagrin. "I said I was only gonna look. I promise I won't do nothin' "—she began pumping him very gently as she smiled up at him from beneath the blankets, her teeth showing white in the darkness—"if you don't want. It's just that, Kee-rist, stranger, you're hung like a Prussian *stallion*!"

As she continued to work him gently, expertly, somehow sensing just how much pressure to apply to keep his blood rising at a slow, even, mesmerizing pace, the pain in Longarm's side faded almost entirely. The dark room continued to pitch around him, but more slowly now, and the cocoon of drunkenness felt like a thin layer of silk over every inch of his body except his cock.

His cock was an exposed nerve being manipulated by a true artist in the craft of male arousal.

He tipped his head back on the pillow and felt a slow smile stretch his mustached upper lip away from his teeth.

Slowly, as the girl's hand moved up and down, up and down, and then she took her hand away and slowly slid her tongue back and forth along his cold-hot, throbbing shaft, his aching, weary, drunken head and body disappeared. And he became only his cock.

She must have sensed that she'd hypnotized him, deposited him ever so beguilingly into a state of utter and complete rapture, because she quit yammering drunkenly and finally dropped her mouth down over him, until he could hear her down there, sucking and gagging and sucking some more.

She moved her head sideways and up and down, and for what seemed hours her wet lips caressed him like oil, bringing him to one degree beneath the boiling point and no higher. Suddenly, with a whispered curse, she flung the quilts back from her head once more and grunted and groaned with desperation as she climbed on top of him, straddling him, placing her hands on his shoulders and leaning forward to position her hot, wet sex over his crotch.

Her hair fell down both sides of his head to brush against his chest as she wriggled around, her face taut with desperate desire. Reaching down with one hand, she grabbed him and held him straight up and then she squeezed her eyes shut and bit her lower lip hard as she lowered her sopping snatch over the bulging mushroom head of his throbbing cock.

A sharp arrow of raw craving slammed through Longarm's groin, and he groaned as he arched his back and raised his pelvis, lifting the girl a full foot in the air above the bed. She gave a little shriek as she jerked forward and dug her fingers deeper into his shoulders to keep from being thrown into the headboard. Ignoring his wounded side, which tingled more than ached, he drove his shaft deep into her boiling core until it would go no deeper.

"Ahh!" Alma cried, turning her head sharply first one way and then the other, keeping her eyes squeezed shut. She shuddered. "Ahh! Ohh! Ahhh, *Gawwwwwddd*!"

Longarm let her do the work after that. She rode him

slow but with a savage fury and when his load nearly blew her off the bed, sending her into paroxysms of screamed curses and shrieking bedsprings, she sagged down onto his chest. In less than ten seconds, she was snoring softly into his neck, his dwindling organ still buried in her snatch.

Longarm's eyes rolled back in his head and he, too, was out like a blown candle.

When he woke, the girl was gone, and wan light the color of oily rags angled through the window to his right. Snow continued ticking against the glass. In spite of the gauzy grayness—a late-fall storm had obviously blown in, and it looked like it might be here awhile—his inner clock told him it was mid-morning. Faintly, he could hear voices downstairs and snores from several of the rooms around him.

He was mildly surprised that his head and his chafed cock ached worse than his side—until he pushed up on his elbows. Then he felt the nasty hitch under the left side of his rib cage, like a good-sized rat was in there trying to chew its way out.

He lay back slowly against the pillow, his temples pounding from the busthead he'd consumed on doctor's orders, and wondered what had happened to the girl. That got him to wondering about the gang—Jethro Mantooth and the boys.

What was their business here in Harvey? Likely, whatever they were up to, and it had all the earmarks of being no good, it was under the jurisdiction of the county, not the federal or even territorial government. None of Longarm's affair even if he was in any condition to do anything about it . . . except bone the gang leader's lusty sis, that was.

Longarm chuffed dryly, then winced at another hangover pang.

He'd just decided to let himself fall back asleep when he remembered his guns. With the Mantooth Bunch on the prod, he'd like to have his .44 and his Winchester within easy reach. The shotgun was over with his tack piled between the door and the dresser. Glancing over the edge of the bed, he saw his holstered .44 on the floor, well out of reach.

With a grunt, he threw the covers back and swung his legs to the floor, blinking against the pain in his head and belly. He stood precariously, holding his arms out to both sides, balancing himself like a tightrope walker, and took two steps forward before stooping with a grimace and sliding his .44 from its holster.

Holding his right hand against the thick bandage the doctor had wrapped around his waist, he slid the revolver under his pillow. Turning again, realizing he was still mildly drunk on the sawbones's panther piss, he shuffled over to the door and plucked his Winchester from his piled tack. He turned back to the bed and stopped.

What about his badge?

If he remembered correctly, he'd been carrying it in his coat pocket, as he never liked to advertise himself when it wasn't necessary. Like coyotes milling around a herd of spring calves, badges attracted bullets.

Holding the Winchester in one hand, Longarm staggered over to the chair against the wall, and reached into the right pocket. Nothing there but a box of lucifers and a crumpled expense voucher. He reached into the left pocket, pulling out only a well-chewed pencil stub.

No badge.

"Shit."

Then he remembered yesterday's foofaraw in the saloon downstairs. Could it have fallen out when he'd manhandled the two Mantooth boys? If so, it must still be down there. If one of the gang members had found it, Longarm would most likely be five pounds heavier in lead weight by now.

Unless, of course, the bunch was in town just innocently cooling their heels, oiling their tonsils, and getting their rocks off over at the whorehouse.

Not likely.

Downstairs, a girl's voice sounded. It was soon joined by the angry pounding of boots rushing up the stairs. "Son of a bitch!" Alma shrieked.

Her brother shouted something that Longarm couldn't make out.

The lawman's heart thudded. Had they found his badge? If so, things were about to get right nasty. He had no chance against the entire bunch, but he'd take out as many as he could before they turned him into a human sieve . . .

He slid the rifle under the quilts, grabbed his Colt .44 from under the pillow, and climbed into bed. As the foot thuds rose in the hall—angry and echoing—Longarm lay back against the headboard, holding the Colt down snug against his thigh as he drew the blankets up to his waist.

Someone pounded on his door twice, so hard the door leaped in its frame.

Chapter 11

Nothing like the fear of death to sober a fellow.

"Who is it?" Longarm growled at the door.

"You awake?" Alma asked, her voice pitched low. Her tone betrayed no more joy than her footsteps had.

Longarm wrapped his hands around the Colt's handle, listening but not hearing more footsteps moving up the stairs. "I don't normally answer questions in my sleep."

As Alma shoved the door open, Longarm began thumbing back his revolver's hammer. He stopped when the girl poked her head into the room, a steaming bowl in one hand, a steaming tin mug in the other.

She offered her trademark smoky half smile. "Wakey, wakey." She raised both steaming utensils. "Stew and coffee. Hungry?"

God, was he hungry. He hadn't eaten a bite since yesterday morning, just after Bone McCluskey had saddled a cloud and ridden off to the great owlhoot den in the sky.

Longarm glanced behind her. He was glad to see nothing but empty hall and to hear nothing more than muffled snores from the other rooms, muffled conversational voices from downstairs. "What's all the yellin' about?"

Alma came in and kicked the door closed. "Jethro's got a wad of cockleburs stuck up his ass." She set the food on the dresser, dragged the chair over to the bed, and moved the stew bowl and the coffee to the chair. "Help yourself. It ain't half bad for Harvey fare . . . this festering canker on the devil's ass."

Sitting down on the bed beside him, she swept a hand through Longarm's hair and kissed his forehead. "How you feelin', stranger?"

"Worse for the wear. What's got Jethro's bile up?"

"Jethro's bile is always up. Nothin' for you to worry about." She grinned lasciviously as she glanced at his groin. "Nothin' for you to worry about at all. I don't mind tellin' you that last night I done felt like I'd died and gone to heaven. *Fuckin'* heaven. No man's ever done that to me, wounded or no. And me drunker than a skunk, too." She reached over and placed her hand on the quilts over Longarm's cock. "But I remember every sweet minute of it!"

A frown cut into her forehead as her eyes rose toward the other side of the bed, where Longarm's rifle made a vague impression beneath the blankets. "You got one hell of a bayonet, stranger, but"—she pulled the covers back, exposing the rifle's stock and receiver as well as his .44, around the smooth walnut grips of which his brown hand was still curled, his thumb on the uncocked hammer—"it ain't *that* long!"

Longarm smiled with chagrin. "When I don't have a pretty little lass in the sack with me, I like to snuggle up to my shootin' irons." He smoothed a lock of hair back from her cheek, trying to put her at ease. "You aren't jealous, are you, Miss Alma?"

She threw the covers back up over his chest and

scowled down at him, a flush rising in her finely tapered cheeks. "You're gonna have to do better than that."

Tension nibbled at the base of Longarm's spine. "What's that?"

"If you wanna keep me from gettin' jealous of your guns, you're gonna have to let me crawl in there and give me a repeat of last night with that cannon between your legs. I'm beginnin' to wonder if I'd just swilled too much of that apron's bear squeezings, and I was just having one hell of a wet dream."

As she leaned forward, Longarm reached over for his coffee mug. "Later, ya damn polecat," he growled. "I haven't had any victuals in what my belly is tellin' me is a month of Sundays." He needed some time alone, to recover and try to figure out what the hell was going on here in Helldorado, and if there was anything he could do about it. He sipped the coffee and smacked his lips. "Damn, that's good!"

As he set the coffee back down on the chair and took up the stew bowl—antelope, by the smell, with potatoes and large, charred meat chunks drowning in rich, chocolate-colored gravy—Alma absently squeezed his thigh. "You haven't even told me your name, you rascal."

"George Long," Longarm said, shoveling the stew into his mouth. The delectable food almost hurt as it dropped into his empty belly. "From over Montana way. Where you from, Alma?"

"Let's stick with you for a moment, George. What did you do over Montana way?"

Longarm narrowed a falsely suspicious eye at her. "Why do you wanna know?"

"Don't get your hackles up, George. I have an idea."

Longarm continued to narrow an eye at her as he

resumed spooning the food into his mouth. There was a crusty bun at the edge of the bowl, and he followed every fourth or fifth spoonful of stew with a bite from the bun.

"If you got nothin' better to do, no place better to go, and *nobody* to go *to*," Alma said coyly, walking her fingers up and down his left thigh and making his cock twitch involuntarily, "I got a proposition for you. Why don't you throw in with us?"

Longarm stopped another spoonful of food halfway to his mouth and looked up at her from beneath his brows. He shrugged a shoulder. "I reckon I'd have to know exactly what it was I'd be throwin' *into* . . ."

"If you have to be so particular . . ." Alma sank down against him, throwing an arm over her waist. "You'd be throwin' into *me* for one thing, and about a hundred dollars a month."

It was Longarm's turn to be coy as he bit off a big chunk of the gravy-stained bun. "Ranch work?"

"Sure. And a few other things."

Longarm swallowed and glanced up at her. "You're not invitin' me to do anything illegal, are ye?"

Alma threw her head back, laughing, then leaned forward and nuzzled his groin through the blankets. "Something tells me, George, you ain't exactly a rider of the straight and narrow path. Now, you want me to go down and talk it over with my brother and the boys? We always vote on such things as the enlistment of fresh . . . uh"—she ran her gaze across his broad shoulders and naked chest—"meat."

Longarm choked on potato chunk, washed it down with a slug of coffee. "Well, hell, why not? Truth to tell, Miss Alma, I was gettin' a mite chilly out there without a roof over my head. I reckon I'd be a fool to pass up a hundred dollars a month . . . if that includes the type of perk I enjoyed last night."

"All right, then," Alma said, plucking his empty bowl from his lap and standing. "I'll go down and discuss it with the boys. Might have to butter up Jethro a bit, let him win some stud money back. You rest, and I'll be up later this afternoon." She headed toward the door with his bowl and coffee cup. "If you hear more yellin' and hollerin' and the like, don't get trigger-happy, George. My brother knows I'm feelin' right tender toward you, and he can be overly protective."

"I'll keep that in mind." Longarm winked his best devilish wink at the girl facing him from the half-open door. "And tell him and the fellers to hold the din to a low roar, will ya? I'm feelin' groggy after that delightful meal. Think I'll snuggle in for a good, long nap."

Alma blew him a kiss and sucked a deep breath, pushing her breasts out from behind her poncho, and went out.

When the door latch had clicked and the girl's footsteps had dwindled down the stairs, leaving only the snores of one man sounding from the hall, Longarm yawned. He hadn't been lying when he'd told the girl he was tired. Fatigue settled on him like a five-hundred-pound anvil.

But he'd decided halfway through his conversation with Alma that he needed to get out and about and try to find out what exactly the gang was doing here. True, he was out of his jurisdiction, and he was recovering from a bullet wound, but he didn't like this feeling of being perpetually hoodwinked by a passel of scoundrels like those downstairs.

They had the town in an iron grip, and Longarm had a strong, dark feeling someone would buy a bullet soon. And when it happened, he didn't want to be lying around up here being used as a sex toy by Jethro Mantooth's nymphomaniacal sister.

Although he had to admit he'd been used in far less pleasurable ways . . .

Longarm dropped a leg toward the floor. He stopped. His head pounded, and fatigue hit him like a runaway ore wagon.

He'd have to grab forty winks before he went anywhere, did anything . . .

He woke with a start to a tap on the door. As he reached for his .44, the door cracked, and Alma poked her head inside. Longarm froze, closed his eyes, and raised a phony snore. He felt Alma's inquiring eyes on him, heard the men conversing loudly downstairs, the thumps of cards slapping tables, the rattle of coins. A cork popped and someone squealed.

No more snores from down the hall.

The door hinges squeaked softly. The latch clicked. Soft footsteps dwindled down the hall and squeaked on the stairs.

Longarm opened his eyes. Candlelight flickered under the door. Cobalt blue light shone in the window, snow still ticking lightly against the frosty panes.

Shit. He must have slept for hours. He felt better, though. Stronger. No more hangover. His side was still raw but he was glad to see no blood on the bandage.

He threw his head back and stretched long and deep, feeling his blood push through his veins and arteries. Wondering how he was going to get out of here—he needed to talk to some of the townsfolk, see if anyone knew what the gang was up to—he dropped his legs to the floor and slowly heaved himself to his feet.

There must be a back door to the place. He hoped it

wasn't being watched and that Alma didn't steal back to his room while he was away.

He dressed as quickly as he could with that hitch in his side. When he'd wrapped his cartridge belt and .44 around his lean waist, he pulled on his bloodstained mackinaw, grabbed his rifle, cracked the door, and poked his head out.

Looking both ways along the candlelit hall that reeked of sweat and whiskey, he saw no one. A low din punctuated by occasional whoops and bursts of laughter rose up the stairs on his left. Hoping there was a way out from the second story, he stepped out into the hall, pulled the door closed behind him, and holding his rifle in both hands across his chest, began walking on the balls of his low-heeled cavalry boots away from the stairs. Most of the doors around him were closed. One was partially open but he neither heard nor saw anyone inside.

He came to the window at the end of the hall and cursed under his breath. There was no outside door and no back stairs. Apparently, the only way out was from the first story.

He turned and started back the other way. Ahead and left, a door opened suddenly. Longarm froze, his pounding heart kicking up some lingering effects of his hangover. How the hell was he going to explain himself?

A kid stepped into the hall carrying a covered slop pail in one hand and a wad of soiled sheets in his other arm. He sort of backed out of the room, drawing the door closed behind him. When he swung around and saw Longarm, his eyes popped wide, and his lower jaw dropped.

Before he could make a peep, Longarm held a finger to his lips. The boy, about five feet tall and around twelve or thirteen years old, had jug ears and wavy, short, red hair and freckles. He swallowed hard, staring with shock and fear up at the big, rifle-wielding man before him.

"Not a sound, boy. I'm friendly."

The boy's thin red brows wrinkled slightly. His jaw continued hanging.

Longarm said, "You got any idea what those rascals are doin' here?"

The boy continued to study Longarm suspiciously, as though he suspected a trick. He swallowed again, shook his head, and hardened his eyes. "All I know," he rasped, "is those mangy fuckers is makin' one hell of a big fuckin' mess, mister. They miss their thunder mugs most of the time, and one of the many coyotes puked all over his fuckin' bed."

Taken aback for a moment by the boy's salty tongue, Longarm said, "There a back way out of this place? From up here?"

The boy looked around, then, stepping back into the room, jerked his head for Longarm to follow. When the lawman was in the fetid room that looked like a cyclone had swept through, the boy dropped the soiled sheets and set down the overflowing thunder mug. He shut the door and grunted as he moved a washstand away from a low, narrow door cut into the twelve-inch boards of the wall opposite the bed.

"This here we used when Pa first built the place, when the Sioux attacked and tried to burn us out. We ain't had to use it for years."

The boy turned a small board latch and drew the door open by a small, wooden knob. It scraped across the floor, and cool, musty air whooshed up from the darkness.

"There's a storeroom at the bottom of the stairs," he said. "And there's an outside door there, too. Watch your step. I was just startin' to clean out the storeroom when them mangy fuckers showed up and started slingin' orders around like me and Pa was their fuckin' whippin' boys." The kid stared up at Longarm. "You a lawman?"

Longarm stared back at him for one silent beat. "Keep it under your hat, son."

"Thought so." The boy reached into a pocket of his worn coveralls and opened his hand to reveal Longarm's silver U.S. marshal's badge. "Found this downstairs by the bar."

Relief washed over the lawman. That badge had been nibbling at the back of his consciousness. "I'll be damned."

"Can I keep it?"

Longarm studied the boy. "All right. But don't lose it."

"I won't."

Longarm drew the door wider and squinted down into the deep blue shadows, barely making out the twisting wooden stairs. "Thanks, son. Keep the doorway clear, will ya? I'll be back soon."

"What if that pukin', flea-bit son of a bitch comes back to his room?"

Longarm chuckled. "I'll have to risk it."

"Good luck."

"Thanks."

Hefting his rifle in one hand and brushing the other hand along the wall, Longarm started down the stairs. Spiderwebs swept over him, clung to his face and hat.

Behind, the door scraped shut, and he was alone in the musty darkness, heading where . . . he wasn't sure. One thing he did know for sure: If any of the Mantooth Bunch found him skulking around, his goose was cooked.

Chapter 12

A low rumble of voices grew as Longarm approached the bottom of the winding stairs. He held the Winchester straight up and down in his arms as he stepped into the storeroom at the bottom. It was cluttered with crates, barrels, gunnysacks, and odds and ends of broken furniture.

The only light was the dusky, blue winter light pushing through the window in the outside door to Longarm's left. To his right was a curtained doorway. Beyond the doorway lay the saloon's main hall from which the clink of glasses and bottles echoed as though from a stony cavern.

Judging by the laughter, the Mantooth Bunch was having another grand ole time. It might have been easier to get a handle on what the gang was up to from inside the gang, but there was no guarantee anyone except the lusty Alma would vote Longarm in. Besides, once inside he might not have enough wriggle room to move against them.

If anyone in town knew what the gang was up to, they'd be the girls in the whorehouse that Jethro and the boys had been patronizing. Now Longarm just needed to find the place in the snowy twilight, then get back to his room before Alma and the others discovered him gone.

He started across the misty room and promptly kicked a crate. The bark echoed in the little room.

Longarm froze, listening. The din continued from the saloon. Cursing his clumsiness—he still felt light-headed and heavy on his feet from blood loss—he continued more slowly, carefully to the door.

He looked out the window and, spying no one around, moved out quickly, pulling the door closed behind him. The cold engulfed him like a giant, icy hand, the snow pelting his face.

He raised his coat collar and moved right along the back of the building, slogging through the shin-deep snow, which showed faint tracks heading from the door to the split stove wood stacked a good six feet high against the wall on either side of the door.

The boy, whose name Longarm hadn't learned, likely had to hustle to keep the saloon's potbelly stove stoked. No wonder he cursed like an Irish gandy dancer.

Longarm stopped at the saloon's west corner and edged a look into the twenty-foot gap between the saloon and the next building. Nothing but blowing snow partially concealing a trash heap. Beyond lay the wide main street. The only lights he could see from this angle were those in the saloon windows ahead and right.

No lights shone in the buildings across the street. No movement out there, either.

It looked like the town was buttoned down for either the storm or the owlhoots. Maybe both.

Longarm jogged across the gap to the rear of the next building. He kept jogging until he was three buildings beyond the saloon, then slogged up toward the main street between two log establishments that were as dark and silent as mausoleums in the blowing snow and howling wind. He heard a cat meow with a start somewhere to his left, but he couldn't see the critter in the darkness.

Near the mouth of the gap, he angled left and hunkered down behind a rain barrel perched atop a boardwalk fronting an establishment whose large shingle identified it as a gunsmith shop. As he peered over the barrel, he glimpsed movement out the tail of his left eye. He swung that way, heart thudding, racking a shell into his Winchester's breech.

He froze, finger taut on the rifle's trigger, and frowned down the Winchester's snow-dusted barrel. At first he thought the figure hanging under the boardwalk's slanted roof, swaying in the wind at the end of a creaking rope, was a deer carcass. Then he saw the square face under a cap of blowing, pewter hair.

He looked right along the street, toward the saloon. Seeing no one moving around, he rose from his haunches and slipped out from behind the barrel, mounting the snowy boardwalk. Holding his cocked rifle at port arms across his chest, he stared up at the hanged man turning slowly this way and that in the wind, the noose around his neck cutting deeply into his blood-encrusted throat.

The dead gent was in his mid-to-late fifties. Small-boned, pug-nosed, potbellied, with a gray mustache and ruddy skin. He wore a white shirt, suspenders, and whip-cord trousers. Plain brown brogans clothed his feet. The man's cheeks were balled, his thin lips bunched. His open eyes were like a doll's eyes, eerie with a ghostly lifelessness as his head turned stiffly with the swaying of the creaking rope.

Behind him, the windows on either side of the shop's front door had been shot out. Bullet holes pocked the wall, window casings, and the half-open door. Longarm peered inside to see mainly darkness and drifting snow partially concealing the windows' broken glass.

Squinting, he saw that the shelves behind the counter running along the left wall had been ransacked, cartridge boxes in disarray, with more jumbled on the counter or strewn about the floor. A glass gun case had been smashed, with only two pistols remaining inside.

Longarm stepped back against the shop's front wall and turned back toward the street. The only lights were those in what appeared to be a schoolhouse fifty yards west, on the opposite side of the main drag. Through the blowing snow, Longarm could make out a bell tower and high front steps rising to a door.

Longarm squinted through the thickening darkness, shivering against the cold. Why would a schoolhouse be lit up like a Mexican whorehouse on Christmas Eve?

Longarm glanced once more at the mercantile–saloon, making sure none of the Mantooth Bunch was out and about. He remembered that Jethro had posted a man at each end of town to watch for newcomers. Would he have posted one out in the storm, as well?

To narrow his chances of being spotted, Longarm hunkered low as he moved westward past the gunsmith shop. He jogged past the gaps between buildings and, continuing toward the schoolhouse, brushed his shoulder up against the building fronts themselves, concealing himself in their shadows.

He paused in front of the school with all its windows lit, then, dropping to a knee and taking a careful gander up and down the street, ran crouching across the main drag. The snow was starting to lay in drifts, and twice he had to slow down and lift his boots high, the school looming ahead and right, lights glowing behind curtained windows.

The cold and the hard walking fatigued him, and he had to fight to keep his head from spinning, fatigue from buckling his knees. He made the west wall of the school breathing hard, shivering against the icy blast of northern wind.

He slogged around to the back of the school. In the snow-stitched, dark blue light, he found another set of steps rising to a door. Longarm took them quickly but quietly, slipping on the snow-slick wood, and found the door at the top unlocked.

He pushed the door open slowly, looking around, finding himself in a large kitchen with a hulking black range, food preparation table, and shelves loaded with cookware and expensive-looking dishes. The walls were freshly painted sky blue, the trim around the windows and doors spruce green. Fine lace curtains shrouded the windowpanes.

The stove ticked and popped with an inner fire, and Longarm quickly but quietly closed the door behind him, closing out the storm and savoring the room's deep warmth edging around him like a heavy, welcome blanket.

In the ceiling he could hear female voices raised in alarm, and the creaks and groans of floorboards as people hustled around.

He moved through an arched doorway down a hall, with a dining room opening to his left and a small but elegantly appointed sitting room to his right in which a piano was angled in a corner. Before the piano were several red plush chairs. On a fainting couch rested a silver flute.

Longarm took it all in with an incredulous frown cutting into his forehead. What the hell was going on here? On the outside the place looked like a school. On the inside, it resembled the home of a wealthy banker friendly to the finer arts.

Longarm was beginning to think he'd entered the wrong building and that he'd have to go back out and continue searching for the brothel that Alma had mentioned, when he came to a large, carpeted parlor at the front. The room, accessed by the front door from which three carpeted steps dropped, was as richly appointed as the music room, with little alcoves furnished with comfortable chairs, couches, and footstools, and a couple of strategically placed brass spittoons. Candles and colorful brass lamps flickered on side tables.

On the front wall, between the door and a large window, was a gilt-framed plaque announcing SCHOOLHOUSE GOLDEN RULES. It spelled out the numbered rules in delicate cursive script, with little red apples residing just left of the numbers. The first three rules were Gentlesness, Quietness, and Respect. Glancing down, Longarm picked out from the long list No Spitting Tobacco on Floor and When Asked to Leave, Please Do So Without Argument.

The last rule was Payment in Full for Desired Services Must Be Made to Miss Lorenko in Person.

Sobbing emanated down the carpeted stairs climbing the room's north wall, near an oil painting of Abraham Lincoln as well as a bare-breasted girl proudly sitting the saddle of a red-eyed black stallion. Abe's eyes seemed to be taking in the girl with grim bemusement.

As voices continued sliding down the white-railed, purple-carpeted stairs, Longarm crossed the room slowly, holding his rifle high across his chest, and began climbing. He took the steps one at a time, his weakness and caution slowing his pace.

He gained the top of the candlelit stairs. The air smelled

of perfume and something else he couldn't identify. There was a scrubbing sound, the splashing of water. That and the sobs and hushed, female voices rose from an open door in the middle of the hall's left wall.

Longarm sidled up to the open door and peeked inside. An involuntary scowl cut into the hard, flat plains of his rugged face. In the middle of the room before him, a pale, naked girl with several gaping holes in her obviously dead body was laid out on a wooden table. Coins had been placed over her eyes, a sheet draped over the table beneath her.

Around the table, two scantily clad girls stood watching a third girl—a woman, rather, dressed not unlike a schoolmarm, with hair pulled back severely from her temples and clubbed behind her neck—clean the body with a sponge, dabbing at the two bullet holes in her chest and the long, wide, savage slash across the dead girl's neck.

The woman cleaning the body had a hard, taut expression. The two watching her were sobbing, one holding a quirley in her fingers. A fourth girl knelt at the base of the room's white wall, sobbing around a cigarette dangling between her quivering lips as she scrubbed at the blood that was sprayed across the white wall and a small oil painting in long, broad arcs.

This girl, puffy-faced, blond hair piled loosely atop her head, wore only pantaloons and a thin, cream wrapper that hung open to expose her pear-shaped breasts. The pale orbs jiggled as she worked, sobbing around the cigarette in her mouth.

The room's two red gas lamps, fluttering shadows over the dead girl and the other near-naked female bodies, lent such a surreal air to the room that Longarm wondered for a minute if he wasn't asleep in his rented bed and dreaming the bizarre dreams of the wounded.

"Kill-crazy son of a bitch," the girl with the scrub brush muttered through her sobs, sniffing. "Why'd he have to go and kill *Cora* . . . ?"

The conservatively dressed woman, likely the madam of the house, turned her head sharply toward the door, to regard the girl on the floor to Longarm's right. "Angie, I don't want to hear anymore of your—"

She stopped suddenly. Her eyes glistened in the lamplight as they held on Longarm standing only half concealed in the doorway.

Her voice was shrill with fear and exasperation as she turned full around to face him. "What the hell are *you* doing here? I told you the schoolhouse was no longer open for business!"

Chapter 13

"Don't get your hackles up, ma'am." Holding his rifle low in one hand, Longarm stepped into the doorway, nearly filling the opening in his bulky mackinaw. "I ain't one of them. I take it they did this?"

The madam, who spoke with a faint accent Longarm recognized as eastern European, probably Russian, had a severe but beautiful face, with slightly slanted green eyes and high, tapering cheeks. "What do you mean you're not one of them?"

"Just what I said. The name's Long. Custis Long. Deputy U.S. marshal out of Denver."

All the girls had their wary eyes on him. The three standing with the madam around the dead girl held their wrappers closed. The one on the floor, however, did nothing to cover her pear-shaped breasts as she twisted around to regard the big man in the doorway, her cigarette still sending smoke up from between her lips. The tears rolling down her cheeks glistened in the umber lamplight.

"I don't believe you," the madam said. She left the sponge on the dead girl's plump belly and stepped forward as if to shield the others with her body, which was full-figured behind the long wool skirt and frilly, white, long-sleeved shirtwaist. "They wouldn't have let you into town, unless you came with . . ."

"I'm the only one. I rode into this bailiwick—before I knew it was a bailiwick—when the pickets were warming themselves in the mercantile." Longarm canted his head to see around the madam's curvaceous figure. "How did this happen?"

The girl on the floor sobbed and dropped her chin to her chest. The others only frowned warily as the madam turned her head to one side. "Maggie, you and Bernice finish washing Cora, then dress her in that lavender frock." As the woman moved forward she said softly, as though to herself, "Cora loved lavender."

Longarm stepped back into the hall as the madam moved out and closed the door protectively behind her, looking up at Longarm with a measuring, incredulous air. "Do they know you're here?"

"In town, yes. At the moment they think I'm in my room over the mercantile, sleeping off a bullet wound."

"And you're alone."

"That's about the size of it."

The woman shook her head as she turned and moved off down the hall. "Then you are useless to me."

Longarm grabbed her arm and pulled her brusquely around. "Hold on there! I'm here to find out what the hell is goin' on in your humble little town. What's got the gang holed up here with their horns out? What're they waiting for? Fancy place you got here, but I have a feelin' they're after more than cooch."

The woman drew her hand back, bunched her lips. The stinging slap caught Longarm unawares. For a moment, his ears rang. Anger nipped him deep, and he had to restrain himself from returning the blow in kind.

"How dare you use such talk, with little Cora lying dead in there!" She spat out what Longarm assumed was a Russian curse, then ripped her arm free of his grip and strode stiffly down the hall, turning at the corner and lifting her skirts above the floor as she started down the stairs.

Longarm followed her, anxiety causing his heart to beat insistently against his breastbone. His time was limited. Even now Alma might be pounding on his door over at the mercantile. Or a couple of Mantooth's boys might be heading this way for another roll in the proverbial hay.

The madam was a strong, resolute woman, but Jethro Mantooth wouldn't be cowed by any woman—excepting possibly his sister—and damn few men.

Longarm was moving slower than the madam, as his stroll through the shin-deep snow had fatigued him. He found her in the kitchen filling a copper kettle with water from a zinc-plated barrel beside the stove.

She glanced at him, the bracket lamp over the stove showing the cool green eyes and copper hair and fine, womanly curves. A damn fine-looking woman. Not your usual dove wrangler. "Would you like some tea, Mr. Long?"

"Why not?"

Longarm stood near the doorway, leaning against the wall, as the woman set the kettle on the range, then pried up a stove lid to drop a couple of chunks of split wood into the firebox below.

"Which one killed Cora?" he asked.

"The fearless leader. Jethro."

"Why?"

The madam straightened, squared her shoulders at Longarm, and crossed her arms on her chest. Her voice was taut with barely contained rage. "Because she showed fear. She would not stop crying, and it enraged him, so he cut her throat when he finished with her, and shot her twice in the chest."

Longarm squeezed the rifle in his hand. "What about the feller across the street?"

"Elmer Black. They killed him when they first rode into town last week and ransacked his store for guns and ammunition. They hanged him mostly to put the fear of God into all the townsfolk. It worked. I haven't seen anyone but my own girls in days."

"How many men here in town?"

"About seven. The others are boys. None of them would be of much use against the Mantooth Bunch, if that's what you're thinking."

Longarm sucked a back tooth and sighed. "That's what I was thinking, all right."

"You better sit down before you fall down, Marshal Long."

Aware that his knees were starting to buckle, Longarm croaked a "Thanks," stumbled over to the table near the range, and sagged down in a chair. He doffed his hat, ran a hand through his hair damp from the snow, and rested his rifle across a knee. The madam dragged a chair over beside him.

"Your wound is where?"

Longarm pointed at his left side. "It's all right. I'm just tired. The doctor dug the bullet out."

"Open your coat," the madam ordered, sitting down in the chair, her knee touching Longarm's. "Let me see. Our local sawbones is a drunk and has been known to do more harm than good."

Longarm winced as he opened his coat. "Now you tell me."

When he had his shirt and coat open, and the madam had leaned forward, inspecting the bandage as she prodded it with her fingers, Longarm said, "You must be quite a woman to kick the Mantooth Bunch out of your house. You sure they won't come back?"

"They will come back," the madam said, straightening in her chair and regarding Longarm boldly. "But I will be ready for them. I have a shotgun in the closet over there, and a stiletto sheathed under my dress. Before they harm another one of my girls, they will have to kill me."

Longarm cocked an eyebrow. "They'll do it."

"I know."

The teakettle whistled. She rose and strode over to the stove where she opened the kettle's lid and dropped in a handful of tea from a blue jar.

"I will change your bandage, and then we will have tea. The storm should keep the Mantooth Bunch in the mercantile for a while, until they're good and drunk."

"I gotta be gettin' back before they find me gone," Longarm said. "I came over here to find out what in the hell it is they want. You have any idea?"

The woman shook her head as she pulled a couple of delicate china teacups and saucers down from a cupboard. "Normally when they come to town, they have their fun and go, in only a day or two. But now . . ." She shook her head. "It is as if they are waiting for something . . . someone. Who knows when they will go? Maybe they will *never* go."

"Nah, they'll go," Longarm said, pulling open his coat

as the woman poured piping tea into his cup. "After they get what they came here for. It would help to know what that was, but I can't figure it. You don't have a bank, and there wouldn't be a stage through this time of the year."

"How would it help?" the woman asked. She sat down beside him, leaning forward to sip her tea. Again, her knee rubbed Longarm's. "They are killers. It is enough to know that. They are far too many of them for you to stand against them without committing suicide. Perhaps you could ride to the cavalry fort and request their assistance."

"*Cavalry* fort? You mean there's still an outpost up by Spring Creek?"

The woman nodded. "It is still there, and it is now being manned again, since the Sioux uprising last spring. They keep about twenty men there. Good Indian fighters."

Longarm sipped his tea. He wasn't a tea drinker but the warmth was soothing. The tea and the news about the fort lifted his spirits. Between his bullet wound, the gang that badly outnumbered him, and the mystery surrounding their menacing presence here in Harvey, he'd been feeling as helpless as a skunk trapped in an outhouse.

"What is it—twenty miles northwest?"

Watching Longarm expectantly over the rim of her teacup, the woman nodded. "There is a freight road. It branches to the right just west of town, near a giant cottonwood tree and an abandoned sod farmhouse."

Longarm swallowed more tea and stared at the polished table, thinking.

"You are not considering riding that way tonight, are you?" the woman asked with an alarmed tone.

"On a good horse, I could make it."

"Look at yourself in the mirror, and then you tell me you could make it. You're pale as a sheet. You need a good night's sleep. And you need your side rewrapped so it doesn't get infected. Besides, it's storming. Even if you were as healthy as you obviously normally are, you and your horse would founder in the draws where the snow lies heaviest."

She sipped her tea and shook her head as she swallowed. "No, you must wait till morning. And if you can't go, *I* will go. I have a good horse—a red stallion—in my stable."

Energized by the prospect of getting help from the cavalry, Longarm leaned forward and rested his hand atop hers. "I'll make it. And if it's all right, I'll take one of your horses. The barn where mine's stabled is likely being watched."

She glanced down at his hand, and the corners of her long mouth rose in an oblique smile. Ears warming, Longarm drew his hand away as he continued to marvel at her beauty. He guessed she was in her late twenties, early thirties, though from a distance the severity of her Old World features made her appear older. Her eyes, however, were alluring, as were the ripe mounds pushing out of her shirtwaist.

"I don't believe I caught your name," he said.

She kept her hand on the table as she looked at him sidelong. "Anastasia Lorenko."

"You own this place?"

"I guess you could say that. I used to teach school here, but then the severe winters drove out most of the farmers, and I had to close." She hiked a shoulder as she added softly, with a faint, ironic gleam in her eyes. "I have done much better as a whore mistress. There are enough ranches around to keep me in business . . . and a stage line in the summer."

"I'm sorry about Cora," Longarm said. "Tomorrow, I'll be off to get help, and we should have the town clear of those lobos by tomorrow night."

"I hope so. But they better not come back here, if they know what's good for them."

From outside came the muffled squawk of snow under a boot. Longarm didn't have time to scoot back away from Miss Lorenko and raise his rifle before the back door flew open and a rough-garbed, bearded figure bounded into the kitchen on a wave of cold, snow-stitched air.

"Well, look what I found!" the man intoned as he loudly levered a fresh shell into his carbine's breech and aimed the rifle at Longarm. "Alma's stranger and the Russian whore! Tsk . . . tsk. Alma ain't gonna like this at *all*!"

Longarm heaved himself to his feet and stepped back away from the table, keeping Miss Lorenko well clear of the line of fire. "Don't get skittish, friend," he said, holding his hands halfway to his chest, fingers curled over his palms. "Alma's got no claim on me, and I got needs same as you and everyone else."

Before he'd finished his speech, Miss Lorenko leaped to her feet, nudging her chair back behind her, and pointed at the open door and shouted, "Out! Get out! I told all of you *out*!"

The man angled his cocked Winchester at the Russian, bunching his lips with fury. "Shut up, damn you, bitch. I don't take orders from no whore. I seen the tracks outside, and I followed 'em."

He bore down on Longarm again, holding the rifle's butt taut against his shoulder. "Jethro and Alma are gonna be wonderin' what you're doin', skulkin' around outside with a storm on when you're supposed to be restin' up from your bullet wound." The man laughed loudly but without mirth. "When you're supposed to be joinin' up with our *bunch*!"

"I done told you what I was doin'," Longarm growled, as angry with himself as the rifle-wielding gang member—one of Jethro's lookouts, no doubt.

"Tell it to Alma and Jethro." The man wagged the Winchester. "Throw them hands high and turn around."

Longarm glanced at Miss Lorenko. She stood stiffly before the table, her chair behind her, her lips bunched angrily.

Longarm thrust his hands above his shoulders and swung around to face the opposite direction. He turned his head slightly. Out the corner of his eye he watched the man move up behind him, holding the Winchester on Longarm with one hand while he leaned toward the lawman's holster with the other.

"Keep those hands high, you son of a bitch," the man said as he reached slowly forward of Longarm's left hip, then slid the lawman's open coat flap back behind the cross-draw .44.

Just as Longarm felt his gun rising from its holster, Miss Lorenko lunged toward the table. There was the loud clatter of the pot's lid flying across the table. And then the copper pot itself was blurring through the air toward the man behind Longarm.

"God*damnit*!" the man shrieked as the pot smacked his shoulder, hot water spraying around his head.

Longarm whipped around. The man had a hand to the side of his scalded head as he held the rifle wide of the lawman in his other hand. He began whipping the rifle back in front of him. Longarm lunged forward, got inside of the gun, and bulled the man straight back across the floor.

The rifle exploded, the slug smacking a cabinet behind Longarm as both men hit the floor with a thundering boom, making the table jump. Miss Lorenko cursed loudly in Russian.

As Longarm rammed his left forearm under the man's chin, pinning him to the floor beneath him, he reached for his .44. His holster was empty. Then he saw the gun coming up in the man's left hand, heard the hammer click back to full cock, and saw the barrel angle toward his right temple, like a snake poised to strike.

Chapter 14

Longarm's fatigue caused the room to sway and his vision to blur. He watched the Colt continue to angle toward him. Gritting his teeth, he cursed and funneled every ounce of his remaining strength into his right hand, which he'd wrapped over the gun's cylinder.

The head of the man wielding the gun was six inches from Longarm's. He, too, was cursing and grunting, spittle frothing on his lips as he continued straining to press the Colt's barrel against Longarm's right temple.

Standing over them, wringing her hands, Miss Lorenko sputtered and sighed and cursed in Russian.

Longarm felt as though every vein in his head was about to pop as he pressed the cocked Colt up and away from him, twisting the barrel toward the face of his attacker.

"You . . . son . . . of . . . a . . . *bitch*!" the man croaked, his blue eyes widening as the Colt's barrel inched toward him. He stretched his lips back from his teeth as Longarm, grinding his own body against the attacker's and keeping his left forearm firmly wedged beneath the man's chin, wrapped his hand over the man's hand, and squeezed.

"Noooo!"

Pow!

The Colt's roar was deafening in the close quarters. As the .44 slug smashed into the man's left cheek, blood sprayed back against Longarm's own face, and he squeezed his eyes closed and turned away as the man jerked and shuddered beneath him. The man's left hand slackened and, as Longarm loosened his grip on the Colt, fell back against the floor.

Longarm scrubbed blood from his face with his coat sleeve, and squinted up at the man beneath him. The blue eyes fluttered and the mouth moved as though the gent were trying to speak but couldn't find the words. Then he farted loudly beneath Longarm and kicked his spurred heels against the floor before all his muscles relaxed at once, and his head fell back against the floor, dead as a week-old haunch of roasted venison.

As Longarm pushed up on his knees, he glanced at Miss Lorenko. She held her hands together beneath her chin, and she was smiling as though her boyfriend had won her a free glass of lemonade at the fall fair. "You *got* him!"

Longarm steadied himself on his knees. One of the girls called fearfully for Miss Lorenko from another part of the house. She told the girl to keep the others upstairs, that everything was all right.

"Only if no one heard the gunshot," Longarm grunted, wiping his bloody pistol off on the dead man's wool mackinaw.

"They wouldn't have heard above the storm. Only if someone else was outside." The pretty Russian crossed the room to close the door, then sidled up to Longarm, looking up at him. "You don't look so good. Are you going to be all right?"

"Peachy. You don't have a slug of whiskey around, do you?"

"Cognac?"

"That'll do. Then I best hide this cadaver as well as I can, hope no one realizes he's missing till morning."

Miss Lorenko popped the cork on a dark red bottle and splashed cognac into a thick pink goblet, turning the glass as red as the bottle. "We will roll him into the cellar—the girls and I." She handed Longarm the brimming glass. "Down the hatch. And then you go."

Accepting the glass, Longarm shook his head. "You're gonna need help—"

"We will need *more* help if they get suspicious of you. You drink and go. We'll take care of that one and clean up the blood. Good as new." Miss Lorenko grabbed a cloth from a rack and dabbed at the splattered blood on Longarm's cheek. "I'll have the horse saddled and waiting for you first thing in the morning."

She gave his face was more brisk rub, then rose up on her toes, kissed him, and nudged his glass toward his lips. "Drink, drink. And then go!"

Longarm slugged down the cognac. The rich, fruity liquor and the woman's unexpected kiss nearly sent him reeling. When he had his feet firmly beneath him, he gave her the glass and a wink, then grabbed his Winchester off the table and opened the back door.

"Tomorrow morning," he said.

"First thing."

Chapter 15

Longarm hunkered down outside the converted schoolhouse's southwest corner. As the wind slammed snow against him in waves, pressing his left shoulder snug against the building, he stared left along the street toward the mercantile–saloon.

Through the howling, snowy darkness, he could make out the lights in the first-floor windows, and that was about all. They looked like the faintly flickering lights of fishing boats far out in a storm-tossed bay, and they were the only lights he could see on all of the main street.

If anyone were out and about in the roaring gale, he wouldn't know it unless he ran right up on them. Doubtless, the gang was staying put. He hoped they were too drunk by now to try a return visit to the schoolhouse–brothel, or to wonder about the man he'd just killed in Miss Lorenko's kitchen.

What's more, he hoped Alma hadn't discovered his empty bed.

Steeling himself against the below-zero cold, he heaved himself up from his haunches and trudged through the snow toward the other side of the street. The drifts were piling up like small ocean waves, some rising as high as the lawman's knees.

When he reached the gunsmith shop, he paused near the frozen gunsmith hanging beneath the eaves and took another careful look around. Then he continued toward the mercantile, not retracing his steps through the gaps between buildings but moving straight east along the snowbound main drag, tripping over buried boardwalks and scattered trash and firewood.

As he approached the mercantile, jogging through the snow, holding his rifle low across his belly, he slipped past the front porch, crouching low so he wouldn't be seen from the two big, buttery-lighted front windows. He could make out the dull roar of voices from inside, see silhouettes jostling this way and that.

No one inside seem concerned about anything but swilling whiskey and stomping with their tails up. Glad to be hunkered somewhere safe and warm and out of the storm while they waited to wreak whatever brand of havoc they were here to wreak.

Longarm curved around the other side of the porch and kicked through the drifts along the building's east wall. He stopped in front of a window and pressed his back against the unpainted board wall, looking around. The stinging wind and snow made his eyes water and scratched his cheeks like rough wood. Doffing his hat, wincing as the chill wind lifted his hair like a brusque, icy hand moving across his scalp, he edged a look through the frosted window and into the main saloon hall.

There wasn't much glass unobscured by the frost, but Longarm could see the table at which Alma Mantooth sat, playing cards with three other gents. The tall, stiff-backed bartender, holding a towel over one arm, tensely deposited a bottle near Alma's right elbow. At the same time, Alma lowered her cards, picked up her shot glass, and threw its contents into the face of the man sitting to her left.

She bolted to her feet and, still holding the glass in one hand, her cards in the other, looked angrily down at the man she'd just assaulted, yelling something that Longarm couldn't hear above the wind. The man—a jowly, bearded gent with an eye patch and a red-and-white-checked shirt under a sheepskin vest—leaned away from her, blinking up through the stinging whiskey in his eyes.

"Pull anymore of that horseshit," the girl shouted, her voice suddenly rising above a fleeting lull in the wind, "and I will personally shoot both your eyes out and leave you to die screaming on this very floor. Is that clear to you, Webber?"

At least, Longarm thought she'd called him Webber. Another gust blew snow like sand against the mercantile wall around him, nearly drowning the girl's voice. The wind died again abruptly, and Alma could be heard once more. "Now I'm gonna sit here and have one more drink while I play one more quick round, and then I'm gonna head to bed!"

She plopped down in her chair. The man to her other side had picked up the fresh bottle. She slammed her glass down on the table, grabbed the bottle out of the man's hand, and popped the cork. As she splashed whiskey into her glass, Longarm slid his head away from the window.

His heart thudded as he doffed his hat. If he was going to get back to his room before she got there, he'd have to make tracks. He ducked beneath the window and jogged straight ahead, ignoring the hitch in his side and the fatigue that rode his shoulders like an overgrown monkey.

He hoped like hell the back door was still open, and that the upstairs room in which the hidden stairs door opened was still vacant.

Otherwise, he'd have to find another place to bed down. But once Alma found him absent from his room, she'd no doubt have all the boys in her and her brother's bunch out scouring the town for him. The whorehouse would likely be the first place they'd look for him, endangering Miss Lorenko and the girls and possibly finding evidence of the man Longarm had killed in the kitchen.

Sucking his own breath back from the penetrating wind and batting his eyes against the snow, Longarm hurried around behind the mercantile–saloon. He held his breath as he turned the knob of the back door. He let it out in a relieved whoosh when the knob turned and the door opened onto the dark storeroom that smelled of the molasses scent of stored liquor and old potatoes and cured meat.

Longarm fumbled around in the darkness until he found the stairs and began climbing, setting one foot above the other, wincing as the old, warped boards complained under his weight. After what seemed a long time, he reached the door at the top—a long rectangular mass of black velvet framed by wan pink light.

Shit! The light meant someone was inside the room!

Longarm canted his head toward the door. Silence. He frowned. Maybe someone had lit a candle and left. His spine tingled when a low, soft snore rose from the other side of the door.

Nope. The man was in the room, all right.

Longarm decided to find out how deeply the man slept.

Taking his rifle in his left hand, he reached forward and slowly lifted the small metal latch free of its hook.

There was a soft click as the latch gave, and the door fell slack in its frame. He pushed it open slowly, grinding his molars against the slight squawking of the rusty hinges.

Inside, a man lay on the room's rumpled bed. He was fully clothed, even wearing his boots, as he sprawled face down on the bed, his head turned sideways on the pillow, pink lips pooching out from his beard as he exhaled after every low, rumbling snore. The room was fetid with the smell of tobacco, sweat, piss, and whiskey.

Longarm stepped into the room, then closed the door just as slowly as he'd opened it, keeping an eye on the man he recognized as one of the Mantooth Bunch. The gent must have been so drunk he hadn't noticed that the washstand was in the wrong place. Probably hadn't noticed the door, either.

Longarm considered returning the washstand to its rightful place, but quickly nixed the idea.

He might need to make a fast exit. And chances were, as drunk as the hombre on the bed seemed to be, Longarm would be up in the morning before the drunk was, and he'd leave through the back door once again.

When the door latch clicked softly, the drunk continuing to snore blissfully, drooling onto his pillow, Longarm tiptoed across the room and opened the main door. The hall was empty, candles smoking in their wall brackets, desultory voices rising from downstairs.

Longarm moved into the dim, smoky hall and drew the door quietly closed behind him. He was halfway to his own room when he heard footsteps on the stairs—the rataplan of boots moving quickly. Alma's sultry, ironic voice rose from the stairwell, faintly echoing. "Good night, fellas! See you all in the morning!"

Longarm's mouth went dry. He increased his pace,

jogging on the toes of his boots. Alma's footsteps grew louder as did the creaking of the stairs, until he could hear her quick, labored breaths. He approached his own door but didn't quite have his hand on the knob when her shadow sprawled across the floor at the top of the stairs, just ahead of him.

Ah, Christ! He'd been so close. Now he'd likely have to shoot her, shoot his way out of . . .

As he removed his hand from the doorknob and began to raise his rifle in both hands, the foot thuds stopped abruptly. "Ah, shit. I forgot my fucking bottle!"

The foot thuds resumed, dwindling as Alma retraced her footsteps down the stairs. Longarm felt all the air leave his lungs in one long, relieved rush.

He threw his door open and stepped into his room. Moving quickly, he thrust his rifle under the bedcovers—she'd think it odd now if he wasn't snuggling with his weapons—and began shucking out of his clothes. He hoped she didn't see the fresh blood on his coat, and he hoped Miss Lorenko had scrubbed all of it from his face, because he had no time to wash himself.

He'd only just shrugged out of his coat and kicked out of his boots when he heard the frenetic thumps again on the stairs and Alma's voice, "Good night, fellas! Sleep tight and don't let the bedbugs bite! Oh, yeah . . . and thanks for the five hundred dollars!"

Alma's laugh echoed up from the stairwell.

Longarm's heart skipped a beat as he slung his cartridge belt over the chair, then sat on the bed to peel his denims down his legs. He was fairly hyperventilating as he heard Alma's boots and spurs tapping and trilling along the hall.

She was singing softly, drunkenly, smug with poker

winnings. He threw his shirt across the room, slipped into bed, drew the covers up to his chin, and turned sideways, putting his back to the door.

The door latch clicked. The hinges squawked.

"George?" she whispered.

Longarm feigned a snore. Maybe she'd go away and leave him along if she thought he was sleeping. He sure as hell wasn't in any condition for fornication, whether she was on top and doing all the work or not.

After what he'd been through—the slogging through the snow, the wrestling match in the whorehouse kitchen—he needed to saw some heavy logs.

Alma whispered again. "George?"

Longarm sent up another snore and groaned a little, as though buried deep in the slumber tar.

The door clicked shut. Longarm pricked his ears, listening. Had she left? Then he smelled the whiskey and wood smoke on her, heard the floorboards creak under her boots as she moved around. By the rustling and strained breathing, he could tell she was undressing.

Damn.

All right, then. Crawl in here if you must. And go to sleep!

He'd already figured that if she was here when he awoke at dawn, he'd tell her he was leaving to check on his horse, make sure the beast was getting plenty of feed and that someone was freeing the ice from its water trough. That would likely convince her he wasn't up to anything suspicious, but the rest of the gang might not buy it. That's why he'd use the back door.

He hoped the rest of the bunch didn't realize before morning that they were missing a man—the picket now moldering in the whorehouse's root cellar.

He heard her shovel some coal into the brazier. Then, "George?"

Longarm concentrated hard on keeping his face muscles slack and on breathing regularly—long, deep breaths with half snores—as he feigned sleep. The bed moved as the girl crawled onto the other side.

"Geo-orge?" She shoved a lock of Longarm's thick hair back from his forehead, ran the back of her hand against his lengthening beard stubble. "You awake? I got some *reeeal* good news."

Longarm smacked his lips and opened his eyes halfway, groaning as though drifting up from a deep pit. "Alma?"

"Guess what?" She sank low, squirming and grunting softly, and buried her face in his chest hair. She wrapped her arms around his waist. "We voted you in. You're part of the gang now."

During all the crazy activity, Longarm had forgotten about that. "Shit . . . well . . . when we gonna have some money comin' in? My pockets is kinda empty."

"Soon, my tall, dark stranger. Soon." Alma wrapped her legs around his and pressed her snatch against his cock. He was so exhausted and fatigued that he couldn't quite believe that the damn thing actually stirred as the girl's silky hair prickled tenderly against it—like a hibernating snake suddenly visited by a vaguely arousing dream in the depths of winter.

"And you know what else?" Alma continued. "I won almost five hundred dollars off the boys downstairs. You need a little extra to get you by, you just let ole Alma know. I'd be happy to help out"—she reached down and grabbed his slowly awakening dong—"if you think you might be able to help ole Alma out tonight . . . Georgey."

Before he could respond, Alma closed her hand around his cock and looked up at him, frowning. "Hey, your rod is cold as a banker's heart. Are you sure you're feeling all right?" She placed her hand on his chest. "In fact, you're cold all over, George. If I didn't know better, I'd think you'd been sleeping in here with the windows open."

Longarm felt a hitch in his chest. Of course she'd feel how cold he was. His blood loss was making him take a long time to heat back up.

Best not to let her think too much and start getting suspicious. Besides, he was beginning to think that even on his deathbed he could fuck half the whores in Deadwood Gulch and even throw in a few more from Dodge City.

He grabbed her arm and pulled her head brusquely up toward his. "I do believe I need a little of your body heat, Alma." He closed his mouth over his. She returned the kiss in kind, pumping him gently beneath the sheets until he was hard as an ax handle.

"Mmhmmmm," she said, kissing her way down his chest and belly. "Now you're talking, George."

She closed her hot mouth over his cold member, warming his entire body instantly.

Chapter 16

Longarm jerked his head up from his pillow. Something had awakened him. A loud noise from downstairs. It came again—an angry bark, then the resounding rake of a chair or a table kicked across a wooden floor. Then there were more raised voices, including what sounded like the indignant squeal of a kid.

Jethro Mantooth half whooped and half shouted, "I'll be gawd*damned*!"

Someone laughed.

The voices dropped to a low murmur before falling almost completely silent.

Blinking groggily, Longarm glanced at the window to his right. Pale light shone beyond the frosty glass. Must be nearly dawn. Good thing the voices woke him—likely the tail end of an all-night poker party. It sounded as though Jethro had either cleaned up or been cleaned out.

Soft snores turned Longarm's head sharply right, where Alma lay buried under the blankets and quilts, her brown hair curling out from beneath the covers and sprawling like a nest of snakes across her pillow.

She was full out. Between their bouts of lovemaking

last night—if you could call it lovemaking—they'd finished half a bottle of whiskey, though Longarm had made sure she'd drunk most of it. He'd wanted her good and out this morning when he got up to start his journey northward.

Slowly, he lifted the covers, swung his bare legs over the edge of the bed. The room's chill nipped him like a volley of Indian arrows. He set his feet down on the cold floor with a wince, then rose slowly, letting the bed come up gradually and quietly beneath him, glancing over his shoulder as Alma continued snoring softly under the blankets.

When he'd removed all of his weight from the bed and Alma hadn't stirred, he sucked a sharp breath against the chill and crouched down to pick up his longhandles from where Alma had tossed them last night in her passion-fury. He was in his underwear and socks and pulling on his jeans when Alma gave a long sigh, squirming around under the blankets.

Longarm froze, his jeans halfway up his right leg.

"What're you doing, George?" she said groggily, turning her head on the pillow.

Longarm swallowed, tried to sound casual. "Got to worryin' about my hoss. Gonna go check on him, make sure he's got plenty of feed and water."

"Come back to bed, Georgey. I'm cooold."

"So's my hoss, girl. Got a cold nature. Got him in Arizona. Just gonna run out and check on him, and I'll be right back." Longarm pulled his jeans on and began buttoning the fly. "I'll stoke the stove for you. When I get back, I'll stoke *your* stove."

Alma giggled and groaned. "Don't take all morning about it. I got needs, George."

"Don't I know," Longarm muttered as he sat on the edge of the bed to pull his socks on.

He stopped, glanced at the door. He thought he'd heard something. When no sounds came but muffled snoring from the rooms around him and the occasional creak of the cold walls and rafters, he pulled his left sock on, then stood to climb into his boots.

A minute later he was shrugging into his heavy mackinaw when a shadow moved under his door. He froze.

Out in the hall, a floorboard squeaked softly.

Frowning, Longarm shoved his left coat flap back away from the walnut grips of his cross-draw .44. The shadow stayed beneath the door—an inky, oval smudge in the brown shadows. He stepped forward as he slid his Colt from its holster and shoved his left hand toward the doorknob.

He'd just set his hand on the knob and begun to turn it, when the door burst open with a loud, thundering crack. The exploding door slammed against Longarm's hand and sent the .44 tumbling through the air behind him.

The lawman had no time to register the searing pain in his hand and wrist before Jethro Mantooth bolted through the door and slammed into Longarm like a bull bounding through a rodeo shoot. Longarm stumbled backward as Jethro turned the carbine in his hands sideways and rammed it up beneath Longarm's chin.

Longarm hit the bed on his back, Jethro landing on his chest and pressing the rifle across his throat so hard that Longarm felt his windpipe pinch closed and his head begin to swell as he suffocated.

As if from far away he heard Alma scream, "Jethro, what in the *fuck* do you think you're *doing*!"

"Think you're smart, don't ya, lawdog!" Jethro's own

red-bearded face was swollen sunset mauve with fury. He bunched his lips and tightenened his jaws as he stared down at Longarm. "Huh? Think you're real goddamn smart, don't ya!"

Longarm wrapped his hands around both ends of the rifle and tried to relieve some of the pressure on his throat, croaking through gritted teeth, "Don't . . . know . . . what . . . the . . . hell . . . you're . . . talkin' . . . about . . . !"

"Jethro!" Alma bellowed, sitting up against the brass headboard. "Let him *go*!"

Jethro laughed crazily. "Don't know what I'm talkin' about, eh?" He gave the rifle one more vicious, grinding shove against Longarm's throat. Then he withdrew the rifle, rose up onto his knees, and scuttled back off the bed to the floor. Standing, aiming the rifle straight out from his right hip, he peeled his vest back to reveal the badge pinned to his shirt.

It was Longarm's own badge stamfald with the words Deputy U.S. Marshal.

Longarm flopped around on the bed, trying to suck air down his badly crimped windpipe and registering the throbbing pain in his bruised hand. He stared at the badge incredulously, awestruck and dumbfounded and ready for the bullet that was surely next on Jethro's list of plans for him.

"Where the hell did that come from?" Alma wanted to know as she hovered in the left corner of Longarm's peripheral vision, hair hanging down both sides of her face.

Jethro ripped the badge from his chest and tossed it to his sister who, as sleepy and hungover as she no doubt was, snapped it out of the air with ease.

"There you go—take a good look at it, Sis. Got it off Halstead's kid downstairs. He was wearing it under his vest, stompin' around real tough-like. I slapped him around a little till he told him where he found it." Jethro laughed again, eyes flashing in the dusky half-light as he glared down at Longarm. "Yessir, you pulled a good one this time, Alma. You done had us vote a federal lawman into the bunch!"

Longarm shoved up on his elbows as Alma glared down at him and three other gang members moved into the room behind Jethro, all looking too pleased with themselves, rheumy-eyed from their night spent drinking and playing cards, and eager.

"Is that right, George," the girl asked softly. "Are you a fucking, ring-tailed, tin-plated badge toter?"

Longarm cursed himself for letting the kid keep his badge. He hadn't thought the shaver was simple enough to wear it on his shirt! "I like to think I'm more of the nickel-plated type," he said, glancing up at the four men facing him with their backs to the open door. His right hand throbbed and his throat ached, but at least he'd gotten his windpipe partly open.

"Never woulda thought a lawdog could screw like that. What a shame." Alma shook her head. She wore a cryptic, mild expression that pricked the hair on the back of Longarm's neck. "What's your real name?"

"Forget it," Jethro barked, stepping forward once more and aiming his rifle at Longarm's face. "What I wanna know is—why'd they send you? They onto us?"

Longarm flexed his throbbing hand and narrowed an eye at the round, black maw bearing down at him. "Who's they?"

"You know who 'they' is, you son of a bitch. Where are they? They still comin' or did you send someone back to warn 'em we was here?"

"Sorry, Jethro. But you have the advantage on me here . . . in more ways than one. I wasn't sent ahead by anybody. I came here lookin' for a sawbones to—"

"Ah, shit!" Jethro snapped the rifle up and turned toward the door. "Bring him downstairs, boys!"

As Jethro stomped into the hall, two of the others stepped toward Longarm. Longarm jerked his right leg up and slammed the toe of his boot into one man's groin. As the man doubled over, clamping both hands over his crotch and exhaling a lungful of air in a resounding groan, Longarm bounded off the bed, his speed and agility surprising the other hombre as well as himself.

He was on the other man in a wink, bulling the man into the room's left corner while clawing at one of the gent's two filled holsters.

"Jesus Christ!" Alma admonished from the bed. "Don't let him have your gun, Phil!"

Longarm rammed his right fist against Phil's weak chin and mustached mouth—two hard blows that sent Phil groaning and grunting and falling to his butt in the corner. Meanwhile, Longarm got his left fist wrapped around Phil's .45. Lifting the gun from the holster, Longarm straightened and began turning, but he didn't get halfway around before something hard and unforgiving slammed the back of his neck.

His eyes flashed like coal-black clouds passing in front of the sun. His knee buckled. As he began falling toward Phil cowering in the corner before him, a stout arm snaked around his throat from behind, jerking him straight back.

He hit the floor on his butt, turning slightly, blinking, to see a short, stocky gent grinning down at him, holding a Sharps carbine in one hand while fisting the other hand until his knuckles turned white beneath the brown, leathery skin. On the floor near the stocky gent, the man whom Longarm had kicked in the balls was curled in the fetal position, spitting curses through gritted teeth.

Longarm sagged back against the bed. Looking up, he saw Alma scowling down at him, her curly hair dancing along both sides of her pretty, oval face. Crossing her arms on her pale, naked breasts, she set her lips together and shook her head like a disapproving schoolmarm.

"You heard my brother!" she shouted, lifting her head to glance at the door. "Get this lyin' sack of dog shit out of my room!"

Longarm heard voices, footsteps, and slamming doors up and down the hallway as the other men, who'd slept instead of playing cards all night, emerged from their rooms, likely wondering what all the fuss was about. Two half-dressed gents grinned from the doorway while the man with the bruised oysters continued groaning and cursing. They stepped into the room and moved around the stocky gent with the Sharps toward Longarm.

Only one wore boots. The other, a long-haired gent with a face as dark and smooth as an Indian's but with pale blue eyes, was stocking-footed. A couple of toes protruded from holes in his socks.

"Shoot him, goddamnit," groaned the man flopping around on the floor. "Shoot him, fer the sake of sweet Jesus, and put me out of my misery!"

The stocky gent with the Sharps glared down at him. "I'll put ya out of your misery, if you don't shut up, Buster. Jethro wants him downstairs!" He looked at the other two. "Each of ya take an arm and haul ass!"

He backed away and canted his head toward the open doorway. The other two each sidled up to Longarm, crouched, and grabbed an arm. The Indian-looking man glanced over his shoulder at Alma cupping her naked breasts in her hands, her nipples peeking out from between her fingers, and the corners of his mouth curved upward.

"Get out of here, you stinking half-breed!" the girl intoned. "Or I'll drill a hole through your fucking Blackfoot heart!"

The Indian-looking gent shared a look with the other man as they hauled Longarm to his feet and began half dragging, half walking him to the door. The room spun around Longarm. He could feel blood dribbling down the nasty gash in the back of his head, no doubt the result of the Sharps's brass butt plate.

That plate made a nasty weapon. He felt sick to his stomach and he couldn't quite keep his feet on the floor. It didn't help that the outlaws were hustling him quickly out the door and down the hall, pushing through the dozen or so men standing around half dressed, some smoking or holding rifles or revolvers. They all looked bleary-eyed, indignant, and befuddled.

When they reached the top of the stairs, not so much thinking as reacting angrily, Longarm lunged to one side, throwing the booted man against the wall and dislodging a candle taper. The man's leg shot out, tripping Longarm as Longarm wheeled toward the other man with the half-baked intention of grabbing the Buntline Special jutting from the man's shoulder holster.

As he tripped, however, his hand swept past the big pistol's walnut grips. His head slammed into the half-breed's belly.

The half-breed cursed shrilly and before Longarm knew it, he and the other two men were rolling down the stairs—sort of like three boys rolling down a favorite grassy hill on their way home from school.

Only this hill was far from grass, and Longarm and the other two gents careened off one another, cursing and groaning, kicking each other and pummeling each other with their flying fists. Halfway down the "hill," Longarm flung a hand out to grab the handrail to stop himself, but just then a spur of the booted man raked his cheek, and then he was continuing on down the stairs, rolling over the half-breed and spying the first floor flying up toward him with amazing speed.

The booted gent tumbled over Longarm and hit the bottom first. Longarm came next, taking the opportunity even in his addled state to bury his left fist in the man's heaving side. The booted man groaned. Just then, the half-breed's left stocking foot smashed into Longarm's shoulder as the man turned a somersault and hit the floor with a grunt.

"Jesus H. Fucking Christ!" Jethro Mantooth shouted. His big, plug-ugly face hovered somewhere in the periphery of Longarm's blurry vision. "Never send boys to do a man's work!"

Chapter 17

Longarm heard himself groan as he stared up at the smoke-stained rafters. Jethro Mantooth's face came in and out of focus from his right, where the gang leader stood, regaling both of the men sprawled around Longarm, the half-breed's stockinged foot resting atop his belly.

"Kindly get your asses up, fellas. I don't want the son of a bitch dead. I need him alive"—clamping a stogie in one corner of his mouth, Jethro glared straight down at Longarm—"till I get what I need from the badge-carrying lobo!"

The half-breed did not remove his stockinged foot from Longarm's belly. He groaned and said softly as he stared straight up at the ceiling, "Th-think my fuckin' back's broke, Boss."

"Oh, for chrissakes!" Jethro looked at the man wearing boots, who had long, stringy, dark brown hair and a long, pale, freckled face. "Otis, get your ass up and haul the son of a bitch to my table. Him and me is gonna have us a drink together, real polite-like, and then I'm gonna get some questions answered."

Otis groaned and muttered oaths under his breath as he

climbed heavily to his feet. Longarm pushed up on his elbows and peered up the stairs. The others were filing down, some chuckling at the pileup on the floor below them, some still smacking their lips and batting their eyes, waking up.

"Otis, somebody," the half-breed said tightly, keeping his limp foot on Longarm's belly, "h-help me . . . fer chrissakes. I . . . I think my back's broke."

Gaining his feet, Otis palmed his .45, cocked the hammer loudly, and angled the gun down toward Longarm. "Shut up, Lyle! I'm sorry your back's broke, but I ain't got time to fool with ya." Staring down at Longarm, Otis flicked the gun barrel toward the front of the room. "On your feet and get over there. You heard the boss."

"G-goddamnit, Otis," the half-breed said, spitting the words like prune pits, "I think my fucking back is broke!"

Otis muttered another curse, slid his Remington toward the half-breed. The gun leaped in his hand, stabbing smoke and flames in the misty morning twilight. The gun atop Longarm's belly jerked. The lawman glanced to his left. The half-breed lay on his back, staring up at the ceiling. Blood dribbled from the quarter-sized hole in his forehead.

"You!" Otis said, sliding his smoking Remington back toward Longarm. "I told you to get on your feet!"

Longarm looked up the stairs again. Otis's shot had stopped cold the procession moving down from the second story. The entire half-dressed crew stood staring in shock and awe at the dead half-breed, one of them muttering, "Dang, Otis . . . what the *hell* . . . ?"

Ignoring his awestruck brethren, Otis recocked his Remy and narrowed an eye at Longarm. "Git up, wolf bait!"

Longarm glanced once more at the dead half-breed. Blood had dribbled into the man's open left eye and was pooling there. The gunfire had braced the lawman. He pulled his heels beneath him and, pushing off his hands, climbed to his knees. He staggered as he gained his feet, feeling a wetness under his bandage and a raw, burning pain. His hand still throbbed.

The fall down the stairs had opened up the wound, and it hadn't done the hand any good, either. But, glancing at the half-breed, he figured he'd come out of it pretty well. As he staggered into the main saloon hall, where Jethro lounged in a chair near the front, his boots crossed on a chair before him, he had a feeling his luck wouldn't hold.

"What the hell'd you do, Otis, ya frog-wallopin' son of a prairie coyote?" Jethro chuckled around the cigar in his mouth, his stout arms crossed on his chest. "Didja *kill* him?"

"No, I didn't kill him," Otis snapped behind Longarm. "I put him outta his misery. His back was broke, Boss."

"Hey, Valdez!" Jethro called toward the stairs. "Is he dead?"

Longarm glanced over his shoulder, nearly tripping over a chair leg as he stumbled toward the gang leader's table. The men were moving down the stairs again, pausing to inspect the half-breed. A couple were chuckling as though at a wry joke.

A tall Mexican stared down at the half-breed, then turned toward the front of the room, shaking his head, his big, black eyes bright with disbelief. "Sure as sheet, jefe. Lyle has gone to the saints."

He crossed himself, then stooped quickly to pull Lyle's Buntline Special from its holster.

Longarm stopped in front of the outlaw leader's table.

"I admire how your boys look out for each other, Jethro. Gives me a potato-sized lump in my throat—it purely does."

Jethro canted his head to one side as he squinted up at Longarm. The man had his burly arms crossed on his chest. "Sit down and shut up. I'll do the talkin'. The *askin'*, that is."

A faint smile played at the outlaw's goatee-sheathed mouth as his cow-stupid eyes flicked to one of the half-empty bottles on the cluttered table before him. "Help yourself to a drink. You look like you need it after that little tumble you just took . . . not to mention your tumbles with my half-wild little sis."

Jethro grinned.

Longarm could hear the others moving up behind him, dragging chairs out from tables and sitting down. Amidst the foot clomps and breathing and hushed conversations was the ominous wheeze of a spinning gun cylinder. Someone was knocking bottles and glasses around behind the bar.

Without his gun, Longarm felt as naked as a newborn babe. But then, the gun really wouldn't help him—not with a dozen curly wolves surrounding him, all now armed. A glance through the frosty windows, glittering as the sun rose in the clear, cold-scoured sky, told him there was a good two feet of snow on the ground. And it looked cold—cold like it got after a storm in these parts. Well below freezing. In spite of the popping fire in the potbelly stove, he could feel it seeping through the walls.

No, a gun wouldn't help him here. He doubted anything would help him here. He should have lit out last night for the cavalry outpost.

Cold blood dribbled out from beneath the bandage over his wound and headed toward his waist.

Holding his coat taut against the bandage, he eased down in a chair. He grabbed one of the bottles and splashed whiskey into a dirty glass. When he'd thrown back the bracing shot, he set the glass down and flicked it away.

"Now, then," Jethro said, "let's get down to brass tacks, shall we?" He leaned sideways, resting an arm on the table and regarded Longarm pointedly. "They sent you ahead, didn't they?"

"Who?"

Jethro studied him for a stretched second. Then he scowled, dropped his chin, and shook his head. "No, no, no, *no*! That ain't how this is gonna go."

"I apologize, Jethro. But you have the advantage here. You know more about what's going on this town than I do. You see, I'm just passing through."

"You don't really expect me to believe that, do you?" the outlaw leader asked sadly.

"No, I don't." Longarm glanced at the silver-plated .45 lying on the other side of the table, amidst scattered playing cards and cigar ashes and a handful of gold coins. Its ivory-gripped butt rested against Jethro's left elbow.

"Now, I'm gonna ask you again, and you're gonna answer me honest-like this time, or I can't be blamed for what horrible kind of fiery misery comes down on you. All right?"

"Understood."

"They sent you ahead, didn't they?"

"Who's they?"

Someone behind Longarm chuckled.

Jethro stared at Longarm from beneath his bushy brows.

Then he entwined his hands together and cleared his throat with an air of great patience. "Let's jump ahead here, shall we? Obviously they sent you ahead. What I wanna know is, where are they? Did you send someone back to warn them that I was here?"

"Yeah," said someone behind Longarm. "That's it, I bet. And then Mr. Lawbones here stayed to have his wound tended. Ah, shit, Boss. They even comin'! They circled around us! Hell, they've probably already reached the damn fort by now!"

Jethro lifted his gaze and dimpled his jaws. "Errol, will you please shut the fuck up and quit embarrassing yourself with your whining?" He slid his eyes back to Longarm. "Is he right?"

Bells were tolling in Longarm's brain, and it was no longer due to the hooch, the wound, the girl, the brass butt plate of the Sharps, or his tumble down the stairs. These boys were either after an army freight shipment or an army payroll caravan.

Those were the only two things concerning the army they *could* be after.

"I haven't the foggiest fuckin' idea," Longarm said, honestly weary.

"Yeah, you do." Jethro spat a tobacco fleck from his lips, then glanced behind Longarm and jerked his head back sharply. "Where are they? Did you warn 'em off or are they still out there somewheres, waiting for the all-clear signal?"

Behind Longarm there was the bark of chair legs hitting the floor, the creak of wood and raspy breaths of men rising to their feet.

"Yeah, that's it," Longarm said, trying to buy himself some time. "You figured it out, Jethro. They're waiting for the all-clear. If I don't give it to 'em, they're gonna swing wide of Harvey."

He turned his head to both sides. Two men were moving up behind him—big men. The biggest of the bunch, in fact.

Ah, shit.

"What's the matter?" Longarm said to Jethro. "Don't you believe me?"

"No, I don't believe you," the outlaw leader said as he rose suddenly, knocking his chair over backward and slamming his right fist into his left palm. "I don't think you're takin' this at all serious. I think I'm gonna have to get you *good* and serious in order to get some serious answers."

Jethro glanced at the two men behind Longarm. Each grabbed one of his arms from behind and dragged him and his chair straight back away from the table. As Jethro moved around the table's left side, the two bruins behind Longarm swung Longarm's chair to face the man. They held his arms up and back, pinning him to the chair back and holding him open like a folding pocket knife.

Suddenly, he became even more aware than before of the bullet wound in his lower left side.

"All right," Longarm said with a feigned air of defeat as Jethro swaggered toward him. "You win. The soldiers swung wide of town. They've probably reached the outpost by now. If I don't get there soon, they'll come lookin' for me. Whole party of 'em likely. Damn well-heeled party, too."

Jethro grinned as he stopped about a foot and a half in front of Longarm. "Why'd they swing wide of town?"

"Uh . . ."

Jethro lunged forward suddenly and rammed his right

fist, knuckle's first, into Longarm's left side, shouting, "I don't think you're serious yet!"

It was like having a rusty pigsticker jabbed into the already tender, open wound. The breath shot out of the lawman's lungs on a long, loud groan. His head shot forward over his belly but it was just as quickly brought back as the two men behind him pulled his shoulders back taut against the chair. Longarm stretched his lips back from his teeth and lifted his chin as the fiery pain swept through him. He felt blood oozing out to saturate the bandage and dribble down his belly toward his pants.

Rage tempered the searing pain rippling through him in shockwaves, and he gritted his teeth as he spat, "You fuckin' cork-headed saddle tramp. I don't know what the hell you're talking about. I just rode in here to . . . *huhhhhh*!"

Again, Jethro rammed his fist into Longarm's side.

The lawman tried to crumple over the wound, but the two bruins behind him held him taut against the chair back.

He gritted his teeth and sucked a sharp breath. His belly contracted and expanded quickly as he panted, groaning, lifting his knees against the nausea and misery, blood oozing quickly now, flowing freely out of the wound.

A figure moved to Longarm's left, and he turned his head slightly to see Alma walk past him. She took long, taut strides, arms swinging straight down by her sides. She turned her head to give Longarm a haughty, bemused look. She pulled a chair out from a table behind her brother, plopped into it, folded her arms on her chest, and crossed her legs.

Her brown eyes honed in on Longarm like twin gun maws, and she lifted her chin toward Jethro. "Don't stop on my account, boys. Personally, I don't like having the wool pulled over my eyes anymore than the next gal. Especially by a lawman." She wagged her foot and sniffed caustically. "What's the matter, Brother? You getting weak in your old age? He looks fresh as a daisy to me."

Several of the men excepting Jethro chuckled.

The outlaw glowered, indignant, his face coloring slightly. He swung back toward Longarm, bunching his lips and clenching his right fist until the knuckles turned white.

Over and behind his right shoulder was a frosty window. In the window something moved. Longarm frowned, squinting his eyes as he stared through the frosty, snow-spattered glass and finally made out the half-blurred procession of a half dozen or so men all clad in army blue and straddling bay horses trudging through the powdery, knee-deep snow.

The soldiers were entering town from the east and moving west down the middle of the main drag—fifty yards from the mercantile–hotel and closing.

Chapter 18

"Still looks fresh, does he?" Jethro growled.

Longarm flicked his eyes from the soldiers beyond the window. He steeled himself a quarter second before the outlaw rammed his fist once more into the bloody, blazing wound that felt like a large, frayed nerve hanging out of his hide.

As the misery swept through and over him like a tidal wave, Jethro shuffled his feet so he was standing squarely in front of Longarm's chair. He held his right fist out in front of Longarm's face, as though displaying the thimble-sized knuckles from which tiny, red hairs curled. He grinned savagely as he pistoned the fist straight forward, smashing the knuckles against Longarm's mouth.

Longarm's head snapped back. His lips were on fire. Blood trickled from splits in both lips.

"That's better," Alma said, smiling and shaking her leg contentedly. "That's what I like to see, Brother."

Again, Jethro rammed his fist into Longarm's mouth. The loud smack echoed around the room, followed by Longarm's grunt. Then, glaring down at the lawman, Jethro said tightly, "You serious yet?"

Longarm slid his eyes slightly to the right, so that he could see around Jethro's frame to the window. The soldiers had closed the distance between them and the mercantile. In fact, Longarm could see only the last two men and the trailing pack mule as they angled off to the left edge of the window.

Jethro must have called his pickets in. Nevertheless, the gang would soon spot or hear the soldiers. The caravan—apparently a paymaster detail—was outnumbered two to one. Not realizing they were riding into an ambush, they wouldn't have a chance.

Somehow, Longarm had to warn them.

Could he endure another punch without passing out?

He curled his bloody upper lip, blinked heavily, and glanced up at Jethro. He chuckled mockingly. "Serious? Why? This a church? Couldn't be. Not with your slutty little sister in here."

Alma quit wagging her foot. Her eyes darkened and hooded. Her cheeks turned pale. An awkward, brief silence fell over the saloon before Jethro snarled, "Why, you . . . !"

He delivered a slashing blow across Longarm's right cheek. The lawman felt his jaw lurch from its socket and heard a couple of teeth crack. He jerked to his right, snatching his arm free of one of the bruins behind him, and, twisting and turning and trying to position himself as well as maintain consciousness, hit the floor hard on his back.

His other arm jerked free of the other bruin's grasp.

The big man nearest him looked down and laughed. "Damn, he looks kilt, Jethro!"

"Yessir, his face looks like a side of fresh-carved beef," said the other.

"Goddamnit, Jethro!" Alma intoned, sitting up straight in her chair and jutting her chin at her brother. "You didn't have to *kill* him!"

As Longarm looked up at them, trying to get his eyes to focus, feeling blood oozing from his face as well as his side, a horse's whinny sounded outside. Then a man said something that was lost on a sudden wind gust.

"Hey," Jethro said, turning sharply to peer out a front window. "What the hell was that?"

As boots began thudding and scraping, Longarm saw a horn-gripped .45 just above and to his left—in the holster of the big bruin nearest him. It was a long-mawed gun, with two inches of barrel poking down from the holster's bottom, near the leather thong wrapped around the man's stout leg.

As the man turned slightly and began moving toward the front of the room, Longarm summoned every last bit of remaining strength. He pushed up off his elbows, flinging his right hand up, closing his fingers around the .45's grips, and quickly lifting the gun from its holster.

The man felt the motion and made a swipe for the gun. "Hey!"

His hand missed. Longarm flopped back down against the floor, thumbed the .45's hammer back, aimed the gun straight up from the floor, and squeezed the trigger.

The .45 roared.

A quarter-sized hole appeared in the lower left cheek of the big bruin standing over him, the man's lower jaw hanging, eyes betraying surprise. The slug jerked the man's head back on his shoulders, and he stumbled away, groaning, throwing both arms out to his sides as he kicked the chair Jethro had been sitting in.

Shocked barks echoed like shotgun blasts as every

man in the room—and woman—swung toward Yakima, crouching and clawing iron.

Most of the men were clumped back toward the bar, only starting to spread out as they made for the front of the room. Gaining a knee and partially shielded by tables and chairs, Longarm fired into the group and heard a yelp as he slid the .45 toward Jethro and his sister crouching side by side before the front door.

"Get him!" Alma shrieked, pulling a steel-plated revolver from the folds of her woolen poncho.

Pow! Pow!

The girl screamed, dropped her gun, and grabbed her bullet-torn right shoulder. Her brother flinched as Longarm's second shot carved a notch high on his left ear.

"*Son of a bitch!*" Jethro wailed, clapping one hand to his ear while bringing up his silver-plated Remy in the other.

The Remy roared.

Longarm heard the bullet wheeze past the back of his neck as he swung to his left, where several of the half-dressed outlaws were storming toward him, red-faced and cursing and extending cocked revolvers or, in one case, a saddle-ring carbine. He sent the entire group diving for cover as he triggered two quick shots into the belly of one man and into the temple of another—both wounded men grunting and tumbling over chairs or tables, one tripping another man who cursed and hit the floor with an indignant scream, triggering his pistol into the side of a candy barrel.

Revolvers barked and bullets plunked into tables or chairs or the wall behind Longarm as, fighting his weakness and nausea, the lawman bolted off his heels and, twisting around, leaped onto a table behind him. Crouching and triggering his last shot over his shoulder, he ran forward, leaping onto the table ahead and left, making for the window straight ahead.

Bullets sizzled around his head like hornets from a pestered nest. One raked his right shin, another kissed nap from his mackinaw, while yet another parted his hair before thumping dust from the board wall just right of the window he was running toward.

Alma's crackling screech rose above the din: "I said, *get hiiiiiimmmmmmmmm*!"

A table sat against the window. Longarm leaped a six-foot gap, landing on the table before lowering his head, squaring his shoulders, and diving through the glass.

Along with the bruised and battered lawman, bullets careened through the shattering window. Longarm hit the downy-soft ground outside on his head and shoulders, and rolled, glass and snow basting him from head to foot. He lifted his head above the powdery drift, sucking a breath of bone-splintering cold air, and glanced toward the other side of the street. The soldiers stood beside their horses, sort of spread out in the shin-deep snow, pistols and rifles drawn, looking dumbstruck, incredulous, their faces obscured by frosty beards and breath clouds.

"Scatter, gents!" Longarm shouted as loudly as he could under the circumstances, with icy snow and prickling glass creeping down under his coat and his shirt. *"You're under attack!"*

The soldiers had just begun to follow his order when, spying movement in the corner of his eye, Longarm swung his head toward the window he'd just leaped through.

A man stood in the ragged opening, his red neckerchief with polka dots flapping in the frigid breeze. He snarled as he extended a long-barreled revolver out the window, clicking the hammer back. At the same time, a heavily garbed figure in a long, wool skirt and with a scarf over her head stepped out away from the wall of the mercantile, and raised a big shotgun awkwardly in both her green-gloved hands. Miss Lorenko grunted as she angled the shotgun's barrel toward the window.

The shotgun roared like a thunderclap. The man in the window triggered his pistol at the same time his face turned beet red. The slug drilled into the snow a foot to Longarm's right, and the man pitched straight back into the mercantile's dingy shadows, screaming, boots thumping loudly.

More shots sounded from inside the mercantile, and beyond the window Longarm could see silhouettes scuttling this way and that. Pistols and rifles flashed. The outlaws were directing their fire toward the street, however, on the other side of which the soldiers had taken cover behind rain barrels and stock troughs and porch corners.

Their mule—burdened with a wooden pack frame and several large burlap pouches marked U.S. Army—ran braying and buck-kicking back the way the caravan had come, snow spraying up around its hips.

"Are you all right, Marshal?" Miss Lorenko yelled above the pops and cracks, sidling toward Longarm while keeping her shotgun aimed at the window.

Grimacing, Longarm heaved himself to his feet. "What the hell are you doing out here?"

"When you didn't show at the school, I came looking for you. Then I heard the shouting. Thought you could use a little help."

"Come on," Longarm said, regarding the broken window warily and grabbing the woman's arm.

He pulled her through a wave-shaped snowdrift running diagonally through the twenty-foot gap between the mercantile and a drugstore. Stumbling as he climbed the snow-laden steps of the drugstore's raised front porch, he pulled her back behind the front of the building though neither he nor she were completely blocked from the windows of the mercantile.

Fortunately, the outlaws all seemed to be directing their fire at the soldiers on the other side of the street, one of whom screamed, clutched his chest, and fell back behind his covering stock trough.

"They're not going to be able to hold them off for long," Miss Lorenko said, yelling and wincing against the din assaulting her ears.

"Nope."

Longarm tried the drugstore's latch. Locked. He flipped his empty .45 in the air, caught it by the barrel, and smashed the butt against the door's glass, breaking out a sizable portion in the lower right corner.

The soldiers were yelling and so were the outlaws as Longarm reached inside to unlock the drugstore's door. He pushed the door open and stepped inside, drawing Miss Lorenko in behind him. Quickly, he slammed the door and pushed the woman down against the front wall, near a hat rack and under a ticking cuckoo clock, and dropped to a knee before her.

"Jesus, your face!" she exclaimed, setting the shotgun across her lap and leaning forward to clamp a gloved hand against Longarm's swollen cheek.

The shots were muffled now but Longarm could still hear the soldiers shouting to each other, their voices sounding anxious and incredulous. A younger man was shouting orders, but Longarm could tell he was uncertain and downright scared to death. It was likely the young officer's first or second payroll detail.

"Yeah, they didn't help my looks any." Longarm glanced at the shotgun. "You have any more loads for that?"

She shook her head and pursed her lips with chagrin.

Longarm glanced around quickly. There wasn't much to the place but a few rough-hewn displays of toilet water and tonics and a long counter running along the wall to the right, with overloaded shelves behind it. The proprietor seemed to sell as much medicine for horses and cattle as he did people. Longarm could probably find some ammunition in here if he looked hard enough, but the soldiers were running out of time.

"You stay here," he told the woman, wincing as he heaved himself to his feet.

"What're you going to do?"

"I've got to get back inside the hotel."

Miss Lorenko frowned and shook her head dramatically. "That's crazy." She looked him up and down quickly, and Longarm didn't like the terrified light in her eyes. "You're half dead, and you've only that one revolver which, I assume, is empty."

"Not to worry." Longarm grinned down at her. At least, he thought he was grinning. His lips and the left side of his face were swollen and numb. "I got more over yonder."

As he wheeled and began heading toward the door at the rear of the store, he called over his shoulder once again, "You keep your head down."

As he went out the back door, Miss Lorenko shouted something in Russian that pricked the hair on the back of his neck. He knew not a lick of the woman's native tongue, but what she'd said had the pitch and tone of a lamentation.

Chapter 19

Longarm's knees buckled. The cold, crisp wind nudged him against the back wall of the drugstore, and he caught himself on a dilapidated, snow-covered wheelbarrow and hauled himself back upright.

How the hell was he going to get to his guns? He had the strength of a sick dog, and he felt like puking. The rising sun sparkling off the fresh snow was like a storm of javelins in his eyes, making the pain bells toll louder inside his head.

The rataplan of gunfire continued from the direction of the main drag. It dwindled occasionally to sporadic, tentative shooting only to rise again to a savage crescendo.

"Hold on, fellas," Longarm growled at the soldiers—far too few to hold off the Mantooth Bunch. If he could get behind the group, take them by surprise, he and the payroll caravan might have a chance.

He hoped his Winchester and his Colt revolver were still in his room.

He sucked a deep breath, desperately summoning what little strength remained in his weary bones, and pushed himself forward. At the corner of the drugstore, he stopped to edge a look up through the gap toward the main street.

Smoke puffed from over a snow-mantled water trough on the other side of the main drag. As the soldier who was hunkered there fired another shot toward the saloon front, Longarm saw the man's government-issue .44 wink in the sunlight a half second before the muzzle flashed again.

Except for one man lying motionless in a patch of bright red snow, the shooter behind the trough was the only soldier Longarm could see from this angle. Apparently, the others had spread themselves widely along the far side of the street. No one appeared to be shooting from any of the mercantile's side windows, which meant he probably wouldn't be seen as he crossed the gap between buildings.

Sucking another breath, he heaved himself forward and trudged heavily through the fresh, deep, glistening snow. When he made the rear of the mercantile, he traced a beeline to the back door. He had to kick snow away from the door's base before he could get it open and step inside, closing the door softly behind him, then leaning back against it to catch his breath.

The outlaws' shots were louder now, and he could feel the reverberations in the floorboards beneath his boots and in the closed wooden door behind him.

"Sons o' bitches can't be packin' that much ammo!" Jethro Mantooth yelled from the front room, his voice nearly drowned by the crackling of window glass and thumps of bullets drilling wood. "When they run out, we'll pick 'em off like *slow elk*!"

Someone else shouted something that Longarm couldn't make out above the din. He put his head down, bunched his lips, and pushed out away from the door, gaining the stairs and pushing himself up heavily, taking the steps as quietly as he could though his feet felt like lead weights.

When he gained the top of the stairs, he threw the hidden door open and promptly tripped over the top step. With a groan, he dropped to both knees. His chin dropped, his head lolled on his shoulders, his eyelids became as heavy as his feet.

He couldn't linger there, or he'd never get back up again. Pushing himself up with an overloud groan, he staggered through the empty, cluttered, smelly room, opened the main door, and took a gander.

The hall was empty, only lit by the window at the end of the corridor to Longarm's right. He tramped out of the room, swinging left and making for his own, the door of which stood wide. His shaggy brows hooded his eyes with consternation. If the hard cases hadn't left his guns in his room, he was finished and the soldiers probably were, too.

He stopped in the open doorway and felt a clean white bird of relief flutter through him.

His revolver lay atop the rumpled bed, his rifle on the floor, its barrel angled under the chair that had been upset when Longarm had groined the Mantooth gang member. He plucked the .44 from the bed and, hearing the sporadic shooting and occasional bellows and shouted curses from downstairs, flipped the loading gate open and spun the cylinder.

Six pills shone.

He flicked the gate home, lifted his coat flap, and dropped the Colt into the holster on his left hip. Then he picked up his rifle. That, too, was filled. Racking one round in the chamber, he turned and tramped out the door and down the hall. Near the top of the stairs he stopped and leaned against the wall, the floor pitching this way and that beneath his boots.

His side was soaked with blood. So was the upper left leg of his denims. With every passing second, he felt the growing effects of the blood loss.

Soon, no amount of will would keep him from passing out.

He lifted his chin and shook his head, clearing the cobwebs from his vision. Pushing off the wall, he continued forward, then stopped to cast a look down the stairs.

Nothing in the narrow corridor but webbing powder smoke.

Longarm drew a deep breath and sighed as he let it out, and started down the stairs, one slow, gradual step at a time. The shooting grew louder.

Ocassionally, a bullet thwacked into a ceiling joist or a wall, or spanged shrilly off a chair or drilled a bottle behind the bar. He could tell, however, that the soldiers were getting low on ammo, for the shooting outside the saloon was dwindling while that from inside was growing more fervid.

The Mantooth Bunch smelled blood and money.

Longarm reached the bottom of the stairs. Turning toward the room, the plank-board bar sliding up on his left and the drinking tables and chairs growing straight ahead of him, he tightened his jaws, took his cocked Winchester in both hands, holding it up high across his chest, and pressed his left index finger taut against the curved trigger.

There were about five men down—some on the floor,

one draped over a table, one angled weirdly across an overturned chair. Most of the others were all hunkered down against the front wall, shooting out from the four broad front windows and the open front door.

The shooting outside had all but ceased, and Longarm could sense the eagerness of the Mantooth Bunch as they, too, by ones and twos, began holding their fire. Jethro, kneeling beside the door, fired the last shot and ejected the smoking brass casing onto the floor behind him.

Alma knelt before the window to her brother's left, holding her revolver in her left hand as the other wounded arm hung stiffly against her side.

As Jethro seated a fresh round in his Winchester's chamber, he drew a deep breath, and Longarm saw the smile lift the outlaw's cheek as he continued staring outside, moving his head around like a carrion-sensing buzzard, his breath puffing visibly around his head in the chill winter air.

"Whoo-hoo, fellas! I think the soldiers are done outta ammunition!" He cupped a hand to his mouth and shoved his head toward the street as he shouted, "You soldier boys ready to call it a mornin'? Throw them irons down and come on out where we can see ya, and maybe we'll kill ya *quick*!"

Longarm snapped his Winchester's butt to his shoulder and drew a bead on the side of the outlaw's head, just above his ear. "I'll be givin' the orders, you cork-headed fool. Throw down that fire stick or take a Winchester pill."

Jethro gave a shocked grunt as he whipped his head and rifle toward Longarm, his eyes snapping wide. The outlaw cursed shrilly and leveled his rifle on Longarm.

The lawman squeezed his own rifle's trigger and watched his bullet carve a hole through Jethro's right cheek as the echo of the rifle's report filled the suddenly silent room like a cannon blast.

The others swung their heads from the windows, jaws dropping, eyes snapping wide. Several shouted, others cursed as their leader was slammed back against the door frame, groaning and triggering his rifle into the floor.

Alma screamed, "Jethro!" as she bolted toward her wounded brother.

"Son of a bitch!" shouted the man who'd been firing out the broken window to Jethro's right, cocking and raising his brass-chased Henry repeater in both hands.

The echo of the outlaw leader's shot hadn't died before Longarm's Winchester thundered once more, and the man with the Henry was sent tumbling back off his heels and hammering his head against the sill of the window behind him.

As he ejected the smoking empty casing over his shoulder, Longarm spied movement in the corner of his left eye. He swung the Winchester around as a gun barked and a bullet seared an icy line across the side of his head, just above his ear. Two men had bounded to their feet and were bolting toward him, one with a smoking .45, the other with a rifle that he was bringing to his shoulder.

Longarm dropped his Winchester's butt to his hip, and fired. As the man with the rifle screamed and staggered sideways into a candy barrel, the lawman quickly cocked the Winchester, dispatched the man with the .45, and continued cocking and firing, cocking and firing, the Winchester leaping and roaring in his hands, the butt hammering his cartridge belt, smoke wafting thick and blue in the air before his face.

The men bolting off their heels and dashing toward him, screaming and shouting and triggering their weapons, were blasted into bizarre death waltzes or punched back over tables and chairs or mercantile display cases. Several triggered weapons as they died, mostly into the floor, walls, or ceiling, though a couple of loud lead bumblebees buzzed past Longarm's ears while one cut a hole in his mackinaw sleeve, tickling his forearm.

Two more hard cases fired from the cover of overturned tables. Alma, concealed by powder smoke and morning shadows, screamed, "Kill him!" Longarm took hasty aim at one of the shooters and pulled the Winchester's trigger.

The hammer clicked, empty.

As the surviving hard cases' guns barked in near unison, Longarm tossed away the Winchester and, sliding his Colt from its holster, ran to his right. He dove onto a table, overturning the table and hitting the floor on his right shoulder. Grimacing as a bullet clipped an edge of the table, flinging slivers into his face, he rolled over, extended the Colt straight out before him, and fired three quick rounds.

The exposed forehead of one of the shooters turned to red jelly while the other man, who'd scrambled out from behind his table to charge Longarm, bellowing like a bull buff running from a cyclone, grabbed his wounded thigh and showed his teeth as he staggered sideways, lifted his chin, and shouted, *"Fuckin' bast-ardddl!"*

He fired his Colt Navy into the floor near his left foot. Longarm shot him through the belly. The man fired his Colt once more into the floor before staggering straight back and plopping down on his ass with a sigh, as though deeply exhausted.

The back of his head hadn't hit the floor before Longarm turned to see a slender, long-haired figure moving toward him from the front of the store. Alma's right arm hung straight down by her side as she marched to within ten feet of Longarm, stopped, and wincing, raised her revolver in her left hand.

"Double-crossing, murdering son of a—"

Longarm rolled as her pistol popped, drowning the last of her sentence and blasting a slug into the floor where he'd been lying a moment before. Flat on his belly, he lifted his Colt once more and fired his last two rounds into the girl's poncho, one after the other.

The slugs sent her staggering back, screaming and triggering her own Colt into the ceiling. She continued stumbling backward to the front wall and careened through a bullet-shattered window, the last of the glass crackling away from the frame and following her outside and out of sight where she landed soundlessly in the new-fallen snow.

Longarm blinked through the wafting powder smoke, keeping his smoking, empty Colt extended out and slightly up from his shoulder. None of the downed outlaws moved. They were spread across the front of the mercantile–saloon in every possible position. The only sound was the trickle of blood dribbling from a man draped over a standing table onto the scarred wood floor below.

The thick, shifting smoke stung Longarm's eyes until tears dribbled down his cheeks.

With a weary sigh, he let his Colt's butt drop to the floor. He took a deep breath and, hearing himself groan, pushed off his hands and climbed to his knees. Still looking around warily, half expecting one of the outlaws to take a last shot at him, he sucked another deep breath and heaved himself from his knees to his feet, staggering.

That anvil on his shoulders had grown to the size and weight of a Baldwin locomotive.

Something rustled at the back of the room. Longarm swung around, nearly tripping on his own feet and falling as he aimed his empty, still-smoking revolver into the room's rear shadows.

The face of the mercantile proprietor appeared in the curtained doorway. The man frowned fearfully. The curtain moved again, and the face of the boy appeared. The kid's right eye was swollen and dark—no doubt the handiwork of Jethro Mantooth.

"You two all right?" Longarm asked.

The man looked around. "What a damn mess." Then he drew the curtain closed, and his and the boy's faces disappeared.

Running feet crunched snow outside and labored breaths sounded. There was the thump of two sets of boots on the porch.

"Lieutenant Briton here!" said a young man's voice from just outside the door. "Anyone alive in there?"

Longarm shuttled his glance to the doorway. A young face capped with a beaver hat with earflaps edged a look around the frame, holding a long-barreled Colt Army straight up and down in his gloved hand.

"At ease, Lieutenant," Longarm grunted. "Only one still kicking—if you can call it kicking—is me. Deputy U.S. Marshal Custis Long." He began tramping toward the door. "All clear."

As he approached the door, the lieutenant stepped quickly but cautiously into the building and pressed his back to the wall between the door and the window. He held his cocked revolver out in front of him as he gave Longarm a cautious, incredulous inspection, then jerked his head this way and that, taking in the rest of the blood-washed room.

Another soldier, this one wearing corporal's stripes, stepped into the room, putting his back to the wall on the other side of the door opposite the lieutenant. The corporal was short and bespectacled, his glasses fogging from the heat inside the saloon. He appeared even younger than the lieutenant who, in spite of his dragoon mustache, couldn't have been much over twenty-five.

The corporal waved his own cocked Colt around nervously, blinking behind his foggy glasses that gave a fishy look to his eyes.

"You took these men down?" the lieutenant asked.

"They were after your payroll, Lieutenant."

"So they informed me." Lieutenant Briton frowned up at Longarm. "I wonder how they knew we'd be here. We change our route and our schedule from month to month, and so far we've never come through Harvey."

"Seems they have a man on the inside. I reckon he knew *where* you were going, if not exactly *when*. You'd better inform your commander when you get to the fort. One of your soldiers is telling secrets out of school."

"I'll be damned," the lieutenant said as he and the corporal continued into the room, waving their guns around as they inspected the dead men.

Longarm started out the door. Feeling eyes on him, he stopped and looked down at Jethro Mantooth sitting with his back to the wall, about ten feet from the door. Though

Longarm's bullet had drilled the man through the face, he was still alive. His chest rose and fell slightly.

He licked his lips and said so softly that Longarm could barely hear, "Why'd you have to come here to git your damn wound tended, ya son of a bitch . . . !"

Longarm dropped slowly to one knee and stared into the outlaw leader's quickly dimming eyes. "The Lord works in mysterious ways, Jethro."

The corners of the outlaw's lips quirked up with a wry half smile. His lids closed down over his eyes, and his chin dropped to his chest. He sighed and expired.

Longarm groaned as he heaved himself back to his feet and out the door. He looked across the street, where the other soldiers were gathering their dead and wounded. One was mounting his horse along the street to Longarm's left, apparently heading off after the runaway pack mule.

Footsteps sounded to Longarm's right. Miss Lorenko ran up beside him, frowning concernedly and holding her skirts above her ankles. "Custis, are you all right? Oh, my God—you look terrible!"

"You know, Miss Lorenko, I gotta say I probably feel every bit as bad as I look."

She took his arm and began leading him off the mercantile's snowy porch. "Anastasia."

"What's that?"

"We might as well use our first names," the schoolhouse madam said. Longarm, leaning on her shoulder, feeling her hand snake around his waist and her breast press against his ribs, let her lead him at an angle across the drifted street toward the converted school.

Anastasia said, "I have a feeling you are going to be here, letting me tend your wounds, for quite some time."

"You think so?" Longarm said, feeling a little lighter inside. If he was going to have to stay up here in this hellish north country, it might as well be in a whorehouse with someone who looked like her. "Well, I reckon you know best, Miss Lor . . . I mean, Anastasia."

DON'T MISS A YEAR OF

Slocum Giant

by

Jake Logan

Slocum Giant 2004:
Slocum in the Secret Service

Slocum Giant 2005:
Slocum and the Larcenous Lady

Slocum Giant 2006:
Slocum and the Hanging Horse

Slocum Giant 2007:
Slocum and the Celestial Bones

Slocum Giant 2008:
Slocum and the Town Killers